D0502227

A NOVEL

★A LOVE STORY★

STARRING MY
DEAD BEST FRIEND

A LOVE STORY

STARRING MY DEAD BEST FRIEND

BY EMILY HORNER

Dial Books   an imprint of Penguin Group (USA) Inc.

DIAL BOOKS
An imprint of Penguin Group (USA) Inc. · Published by The Penguin Group

Penguin Group (USA) Inc., 375 Hudson Street, New York, NY 10014, U.S.A. · Penguin
Group (Canada), 90 Eglinton Avenue East, Suite 700, Toronto, Ontario, Canada M4P
2Y3 (a division of Pearson Penguin Canada Inc.) · Penguin Books Ltd, 80 Strand, London
WC2R 0RL, England · Penguin Ireland, 25 St. Stephen's Green, Dublin 2, Ireland (a
division of Penguin Books Ltd) · Penguin Group (Australia), 250 Camberwell Road,
Camberwell, Victoria 3124, Australia (a division of Pearson Australia Group Pty Ltd) ·
Penguin Books India Pvt Ltd, 11 Community Centre, Panchsheel Park, New Delhi - 110
017, India · Penguin Group (NZ), 67 Apollo Drive, Rosedale, North Shore 0632, New
Zealand (a division of Pearson New Zealand Ltd) · Penguin Books (South Africa) (Pty)
Ltd, 24 Sturdee Avenue, Rosebank, Johannesburg 2196, South Africa · Penguin Books
Ltd, Registered Offices: 80 Strand, London WC2R 0RL, England

1 3 5 7 9 10 8 6 4 2

Library of Congress Cataloging-in-Publication Data
Horner, Emily.
A love story starring my dead best friend / by Emily Horner.
p. cm.
Summary: As she tries to sort out her feelings of love,
seventeen-year-old Cass, a spunky math genius with an introverted streak,
finds a way to memorialize her dead best friend.
ISBN 978-0-8037-3420-3 (hardcover)
[1. Friendship—Fiction. 2. Interpersonal relations—Fiction. 3. Sexual orientation—
Fiction. 4. Love—Fiction. 5. Lesbians—Fiction.] I. Title.

PZ7.H7828Lo 2010
[Fic]—dc22
2009023820

To Beth,
who has taught me
much about writing,
and friendship

Dear Julia,

I'm writing this because I still turn around whenever I hear your name, and I just turned around.

This Julia is eight years old. She's in the booth behind me with her mother and father and older brother. She has just visited the orthodontist, and there is nothing in this world that could console her. Certainly not the promise of being able to chew gum again someday. I want to tell her that it's going to be okay, except that for the last two months people have been telling me it's going to be okay, and they are all wrong and I want to bite their heads off.

I'm writing this on a napkin at a hot dog place outside a town called Dwight, Illinois. As long as days last in the middle of June, I was still surprised when the sun started to go down and I looked at my watch and it was eight o'clock already. Fifty-some miles on my bike today, and I'd better start looking for somewhere to spend the night.

I am going to California, just like we planned. I'm riding my bicycle there, and I know it's an impossible distance—the rest of Illinois, Missouri, Oklahoma, Texas, New Mexico, Arizona, California. I've been doing the math, on napkins or in notebooks, to make it look like less of an impossible distance. I've got 2,391 miles left now, and that's not a number that means anything, but the precision is comforting.

Seventy-nine days between today and the last day of August, when I'd better get on a bus back home before school starts. Divide it out, you get a little more than thirty miles a day, and there's something reassuring about the calculations. Like how we always did it when one of us was freaking out that we would never have time to write that fifteen-page paper, or never be able to save up enough for decent seats at the theater. It makes it look possible. It makes me forget that I can't do this and I don't expect to.

But somehow, it's real. My mother gave me a cell phone and a credit card and sunscreen, and I am prepared for anything that could conceivably happen. And condoms, also. I can see the theoretical value in being prepared for anything, but—I just wish that you were here so I could laugh it off and make some bad joke about that being about as necessary as a zombie contingency plan. Instead of thinking about what I can't bring myself to say.

Of course I do have a zombie contingency plan. You know how Jon wants everybody to have zombie contingency plans.

I don't know whether I should call Oliver back. I pick up the phone and I can't do it.

I don't even know what I should do with this letter, because I'm writing as if there was somebody I could send it to, and there's not.

There's just this Tupperware box in the pannier

of my bike, and it's so light. So terribly light, with nothing in it but your ashes, but it's not light at all. Whenever I think about it, I can barely move.

And yet somehow I keep moving, because it's just me perched on twenty pounds of steel in motion, with infinite possibilities stretching out in front of me, a vastness that gives me vertigo. The heat on my forearms, and the wind in my hair sweeping in through the helmet vents, and the resistance against my legs as I shift the gears down to muscle myself up the hill. It turns my whole existence into my legs pedaling, my body leaning into the turns, my fingers on the brakes, my eyes on the street. It is so fast and beautiful and all-consuming that my brain doesn't have room for anything else, and I like it that way. It means I don't have to think about you.

But I do anyway.

What I am thinking, when this all looks pointless and hopeless and dumb, is that you haven't seen the ocean yet.

I'm going to shove myself up these hills. I'm going to sleep on hard ground in my little tent. I'm going to show you the ocean.

You'll be waiting for me there, yeah?

NOW

I spent the summer with the smells of rain and grass and sky, and the horizon stretching out for ten miles in front of me. The basement workshop was a foreign country now, with blood and rust and sawdust in the air, and fluorescent lights that popped and flickered, and air-conditioning that made me shiver and rub my shoulders even though it was the middle of August. But I was alone with my thoughts, like I'd been all summer, and that was fine by me.

In front of me I had the sketches that Lissa drew, and an entire book of Japanese architecture marked up with

Amy's sticky notes to show how the castle and the shrine were supposed to look. But I started with something simple, marking the contours of the wood cut-outs that were supposed to stand in for bushes. Ruler, protractor, French curves.

I fell into concentration and wasn't sure how much time had passed when I heard a voice say "Hey" from the stairs.

"Hey," I said. I glanced up, but I couldn't see anything more than a pair of feet from where I was.

"I was going to do some sewing down here, is that cool?"

"It's cool."

"Got some music, if you want. No show tunes."

"Thank God."

She came into view little by little—white and pink sneakers. Tights striped in rainbows. A black skirt that puffed out at the sides. A tiny girl, barely five feet, her hair tied back with a lime green scrunchie—she looked as if she'd come right out of the halls of middle school. And it was too late to say no, it was not cool, please go away.

"Heather." I said it like I was expecting her to say, *No, I'm Heather's good twin.*

"Guilty as charged." With barely a nod, she sat down over in the empty seat by the stereo and handed me the CD wallet. "Choose something."

She'd hardly said a sentence to me and already I was

freezing up and wishing I could throw the CDs at her. I would've been ashamed to pick a fight over it. She hadn't done anything wrong except waltz in pretending not to know me, as if there wasn't any history between us. But I wasn't going to go pawing through her CD collection so that we could have a secret musical soulmates thing just because we both liked Arcade Fire. So I handed it back to her.

The first song sounded of suicidally depressed fine gravel. She started sewing; I went back to my pencils and plywood. All we had to do was be civil to each other. We only had to hang out in the same room for a while, hang out with the same friends for a while, and when the play was over we'd be able to get lost from each other in the high school crowds. In the middle of two thousand students, you should be able to avoid the one you can't stand, even if you are both rabid over-achievers. Oliver told me as much, more than I wanted to hear, and when she was sitting across from me, small and harmless with needle and thread, I could almost believe it.

She stopped the disc to put in a different one. "Maybe something just a teeny bit more cheerful." Some bouncy jangling guitars came on, but I only heard about half a verse before she stopped that too.

Quiet again. She looked me in the eye. "We'd better talk."

The folding chair where I was sitting creaked as I

swiveled around. "Can we just ignore each other like we were supposed to?"

"I want a truce."

"A truce." I repeated it back to her, not really believing it.

"We have got to be civil to each other for Oliver and Jon and Lissa and Amy and everybody. You probably know that better than I do. I'm not going to quit working on this play, because I make a damn fine ninja princess, and you're not going to quit, so. As far as I can see, we don't have much choice."

"Does this look like open warfare to you?"

"Well, no." She chewed on her lip. "But look at the Cold War. Everything's all frosty and sort of polite, but the minute you make three wrong steps—poof, you've got nuclear winter. You can already hear everyone trying to walk on glass, you know? Like everyone's going to start yelling at everyone if someone says the wrong thing. I mean, Ollie is—" She shook her head. "Well, you know."

Yeah. He'd lost his girlfriend. He was barely holding it together.

Three years since the last time I saw her, and you'd think that time would heal things. Maybe it should have; maybe it would have, if only Julia were here, if only I didn't have to handle it by myself. Julia should have been in the basement with me right now, rehearsing her ninja princess lines. That's why I left in the first place.

I'd agreed to be here, though. I'd tried to run away from it and I was done running now. Heather didn't know how much I owed to Oliver. She didn't know that I wouldn't quit now even if she turned on the viciousness I remembered. I was doing this for him—and for Julia, of course. Heather had nothing to do with it.

"You get yourself cast as the lead in my dead best friend's play, fine. You take the closest thing to friends I've got, fine. But you expect us to be all chummy to each other, when I haven't even heard you say you're sorry?"

"I'm not saying it now," she said. "It's too cheap to apologize and not be able to give you an explanation. And it's even worse if I *do* give you an explanation. Oh, feel my pain! I am entitled to get away with all the stupid stuff I pulled because no one understood me!" She put her hand over her chest and struck a dramatic pose.

"Yeah, it's cheap. But you've given me *nothing* so far, and I still wouldn't trust you as far as I could throw you."

"Bet you could throw me pretty far, though."

She sat down in front of me, legs crossed, elbows on her knees, tugging at her skirt to keep it modest. From up close, I could see the Hello Kitty designs on her sneakers. "So I'm not going to apologize. Yet. I'm just going to say, a lot can change in three years. Go on that for now. I've seen your glitter-painted anti-war signs. Aren't you supposed to be the kind of person who'd make peace with Satan himself?"

9

Don't even try that if-you-were-really-a-Quaker thing.

"Satan didn't call me a dyke in front of the whole school."

"I bet he would have. He's mean like that." She smirked a little, the kind of smile that has begging and pleading hidden underneath it, and an apology too: mean like that. It was probably as much as I could hope for.

"Look, Cassandra . . . I'm not asking you to be my friend, or even pretend to be my friend. Actually, please don't pretend to be my friend. I had enough of that last year. I'm sick of it. You'll be doing the backstage stuff, I'll be rehearsing, so we'll barely even have to look at each other."

"So basically we can ignore each other. Like we were going to do anyway."

"Exactly. But I wanted to formalize this whole process of ignoring each other."

"You've been thinking about this for a while."

"I figured you were going to come back eventually."

She was right, and I knew it, and she knew it, but it still stuck in my throat. "Can I ask you something?"

"What?"

"How come you're transferring back to public school?" Which is to say, my turf, the place where I was safe from you. Heather had transferred to St. Joseph's after middle school. You don't just switch schools when you're about to start your senior year. It's too many people, too many memories, to leave behind.

"Later," she said, at the sound of stomping on the stairs. "I gotta go rehearse. You wouldn't want to come up and watch, would you?"

I shook my head. I hadn't even worked up the courage to read the play yet—to see everything that was Julia's in her words. And her ninja bloodshed too. I'd never been good with violence, which is why Amy thought it was hilarious to show me all the disgusting stuff she found on underground YouTube knockoffs, but it was unbearable when I was still getting used to the idea that death was something that could happen to real people. "Too much work to do down here. We've only got a month to get everything finished, and after school starts I'm not going to have any time."

"Suit yourself," she said with a shrug. "I think you'd like it, though."

As if she knew anything about me and what I'd like.

And then, not half an hour later, Lissa yelled down the stairs, "You've gotta come up and watch this. *No* is not an optional answer. *Later* is not an optional answer. Understand?"

So I dragged myself up the stairs and into the theater. It was just Amy, Lissa, and Jon on stage, no costumes, nothing resembling a set, no instruments to back them up, but Lissa started off singing:

I bet you think you're smart
And you think you've got skills
Amy next:
You might be going to Harvard,
But I bet I've got more kills
And Jon:
If you think there's no ninjas in our midst
It's just because we vanish into mist ...

Then, three-part harmony in soprano, alto, and tenor as they launched into the chorus:

Ninjas can divide by zero
We never break a bone
And we never cry for home
And our awesome stealth is known across the world—

(It's not stealth if you're famous for it), Lissa said. *(Oh, whatever)*, Amy said.

Ninjas can divide by zero
And I just want to remind
There's a ninja right behind
Your seat—no don't look! There he went!
Ninjas can divide by zero
So if you didn't know
You better stay and watch the show

Or else we'll all flip out and chop you into numerous
small bloody pieces because that's what ninjas do.

Wow.

In March I'd missed a problem on a math test because I'd gotten careless and divided by zero. Not a big
deal, to get a 95, but it was such a stupid mistake, and
Julia had tried to console me. "Ninjas can divide by
zero," she said.

"No they can't."

"And why not? Ninjas can do lots of stuff."

"Because it's not a matter of having lots of skills. It's
mathematically impossible. There would have to be
some number that you could multiply by zero to get a
non-zero number, and there isn't. It doesn't work."

"Maybe there is such a number and it's just being
stealthy," Julia had said, and it was dumb but it gave me
a mental image of numbers dressed in black hiding in
the woods, and that made things better.

And now that little inconsequential moment, that moment that I barely even remembered, was in this song,
in this play.

I didn't know whether to laugh or cry. With Heather
a couple rows behind me, all I could do was bite my
cheek and look the other way. I wasn't going to make
myself a target again.

. . .

Heather and I spent two more days in the basement workshop, not talking and hardly even glancing at each other, and then Ollie called everybody up for a meeting in one of the theater's little classrooms—hardly more than an ancient scratched coffee table surrounded by a few seats. We looked at each other like we were both waiting for the other one to sit down first, still not quite ready to declare peace. Finally I couldn't take it anymore and slouched down on the scarred magenta beanbag chair, and Heather perched on the arm of the old couch where Ollie, Lissa, and Jon were already sitting. Amy glanced from Heather to me and back again, blinking sharply. And then, when the silence threatened to stretch out unbearably, she said, "So, I know I said I wasn't going to see *The Ossuary 2* because the original was just a lame rip-off of a decent Korean gorefest, but I was really bored last night, and of course they had to cut out all the weird dark humor. And they put in this dumb plotline about the hero's dysfunctional family, and how his alcoholic mother walked out on him and he had to raise his little brother himself, and the little brother got in with a bad crowd and ended up in a gang and then he got shot and that's why he's a creepy dead guy. Which is much less interesting than the war dead in the original."

Sometimes people had to remind Amy of the difference between inside thoughts and outside thoughts, but that was the exact right thing to say. Jon started to argue with her about exactly how bad the movie was, and I just leaned back and ran my hands over the bookshelves of beat poets and Stephen King and V. C. Andrews that had been left by another generation of theater geeks. But then Ollie stood up, and we all settled down and waited for the meeting part of the meeting to start. He rubbed the back of his neck and looked down as if he didn't want to be in charge, didn't want to be six feet tall and practically a senior.

"Lissa, costume status?"

"The sewing machine is off limits to all the freshninjas, as of now," she said. "One of them who will remain nameless just wrecked three yards of the cheap satin, which, I will admit, is a royal pain to sew. And that goes for you too, Heather, freshninja or not."

I raised a hand, embarrassed at always being four steps behind on their inside jokes, embarrassed at having been away so long that I didn't know what was going on anymore.

"We had way too many volunteers," Lissa explained. "Mostly freshmen who didn't have anything better to do with their summers, hence freshninjas. So we picked the ones who promised to pull their weight with the technical stuff. We'd be even more behind schedule than we are, otherwise."

"Not really," Amy said. "It's all I can do trying to herd a pack of fourteen-year-olds who were raised by wolves, and who think that the proper use of a bucket of paint is to pour it over someone's head."

"Like you've never poured a bucket of paint over someone's head," Oliver said.

"You were there. You knew he had it coming."

Oliver started to smile, but covered his mouth, shaking his head in resignation. "So we have tons of problems, and nothing that's news. Right?"

Nods all around.

"And I guess everybody knows what they're supposed to be doing except for Cass."

"I do know what I'm supposed to be doing," I said. "Right?" The kind of grunt work I'd always volunteered myself for. Or gotten myself volunteered for. Building sets, painting them, maybe helping with the lights if they didn't have anyone better. Unless they didn't need me because they had enough freshninjas for the technical parts.

"Did you read the play yet?"

"No," I admitted. "I know, you gave it to me ages ago, I'm getting to it, really, but it's not like I have a part—"

"But you do—in act three. The whole castle has to be booby-trapped. It's like the Temple of Doom on a lunch-money budget. And you are in charge of it. It's in the script that way."

"Me."

"Who else is going to do it?"

"Well, I—"

"Why do you think Julia wrote it in? Look, she wrote a part for the flamboyant gay guy, she wrote a part for the good-looking tenor, and she wrote a part for the girl who can do calculus in her head. This is all math and physics, and no one else could get it right."

"Come on. Nobody can do calculus in their head." Okay, so I was a mathlete. So I had joked to Julia sometimes during physics class that the point of physics was to calculate trajectories for catapults—catapults would make cafeteria food fights so much more sophisticated, after all.

"I don't know if I should be building weapons," I said, not so much because it was true as because I was a little overwhelmed. "Lissa—you know what I mean, right?"

She shrugged. "I may not believe in killing animals, but you have to admit, sometimes human beings have it coming. Especially fictional ones. It's not as if anyone's actually going to get hurt."

I thought about this. I was just this girl who hung around the theater geeks and pretended to know what they were talking about, and didn't even care except that if Julia was around I'd be happy to paint some sets or figure out the lights. It made me feel good, wanted. How much had she known about that?

"You don't have to do it," Ollie said.

But I was already gnawing on things in my mind—how am I going to make this? Wouldn't it be cool if I could put in some crossbows? Did they have crossbows in feudal Japan? Could I maybe hide some shurikens inside the walls? Did we care about historical accuracy, considering that we were making a musical about ninjas?

All I said was, "I can handle it."

Even Heather had stopped mattering to me, for a minute or two. I was too busy chasing one thought after another, grinning inside at the thought of unleashing my special effects upon the school auditorium. And grinning because Julia planned things out this way.

Administrative odds and ends kept the meeting going, conversations I couldn't understand. They'd been doing this all summer while I'd been away; they had their own shorthand. But after a while we started putting away our sketches and papers, and people started drifting to their separate tasks or their weekend plans. Heather left, and then I looked around and she was there again.

"Cassandra? I saw your bike outside."

"Yes, I'm riding the same bike I had in middle school. Very funny."

"Listen," she said, "if you need a ride to the home improvement store, I've got plenty of cargo space."

I started to say that I was fine, I didn't need it, but the home improvement store was way on the edge of town, never an easy ride—and not now, with the pink bike that I'd outgrown a couple inches ago, that lacked the rack trunk and panniers that would have made hauling cargo a lot easier. Not when I'd have to figure out how to balance with lumber strapped to the seat with a bungee cord. And I was sparking with the energy of having a fun and interesting job to do, the kind of energy that makes you want to pounce on a job right away without making a plan or waiting for everything to line up perfectly.

"Yeah," I said. "Yeah, actually, I kind of do."

I looked at her, trying to find something on the surface that would tell me who she was and why she did anything she did, and I couldn't even begin to guess at her motives, or figure out whether or not I could put even a thread of trust in her. But she just shrugged and started to walk to her car, waving me forward over her shoulder.

I took the front wheel off my bike and loaded it into the trunk of her little black SUV, and we were off. For a while we didn't talk, and Heather spun between the radio stations so that we would have something to break the silence.

"So, are you ever going to explain why you're not going back to St. Joseph's next year?"

"Oh, you know Catholic schools. The gangs, the drugs, the violence."

"No, really."

Quiet. "Aw, hell," she said in the end. "I guess I have to start somewhere. Have you ever had one of those breakups that is so boiling-in-oil painful that you can't even stand to go to the same school anymore, lest you catch a glimpse of their face in the hallway and start crying all over your math test?"

"No," I said honestly. "But I get the running away from your problems part. It's stupid, though, right? They always end up following us around anyway."

I looked over at Heather, her head silhouetted in the driver's-side window, resting just for a moment on her outstretched fingertips. "It doesn't work?"

"Well," I said ruefully, "maybe next time I'll try something faster than a bike."

THEN

Months before Heather came back from St. Joseph's, months before Julia died and I got it into my head to ride my bike to California, it was just a normal winter. A normal Saturday night in February, when Jon picked *Rent* and Amy picked *Zatoichi: The Blind Swordsman* and we watched them back to back on the big screen in Ollie's basement. It didn't feel portentous. It didn't feel like the beginning of something.

Oliver and Julia curled up on the couch, heads together, nuzzling each other in the show-offy way high school couples have; Amy had her perch on the computer chair where she could look up movie trivia; Lissa was standing by the doorway in a T-shirt that had been stitched together out of three different ones, stirring cookie batter and defying anyone to call her domestic. Jon and I were lying on our stomachs in front of the TV, sharing a bag of Cheez Doodles. A merlot from Ollie's parents' wine cellar was going around too—that, the big-screen TV, and the grand piano were the main reasons we usually hung out at Ollie's. I think the merlot is some explanation for what happened after we had watched the movies and flicked through all the commentary that we wanted to see.

Julia sat up and declared, quietly and sincerely, "There should be a musical about ninjas."

"Sweet," Ollie replied.

"And there would be a song called 'Seasons of Blood.'"

Then, of course, someone started singing it.

When Julia was fourteen, she went away to drama camp for a summer. That was the summer after eighth grade, the summer after we'd decided that neither one of us would ever be cool, or popular, but we could at least stick together. She came back an inch taller and bubbly in a way she'd never been before—and all of a sudden she had friends. That first day of high school, she dragged me to the theater nerds' lunch table and introduced me to everybody she'd met over the summer and cracked jokes and talked about the auditions next week, while I sat there quiet and anxious. They crowned Julia Queen of the Nerds, and no wonder: She was brilliant with lyrics and a melody. She had written odes to the school attendance policy, the ancient physics teacher, the swim team (whose record was an astonishing 0–9), and Newtonian mechanics, all in notes passed during eighth-period physics.

It was normal for them to burst into song, to toss little pieces of a melody around like a game of four square, bouncing from one person to the next. It was disconcertingly like living in a Broadway musical. But then there was me, the one who couldn't even carry a tune, and I didn't have anything to say. By sophomore year, I'd started to wonder if someday I wouldn't have anything to say to Julia at all.

We'd been friends since third grade, when my parents had finally given up trying to pretend it was bohemian and edgy to live in the slightly scary part of Chicago and moved to the suburbs. Even then there was a line between the kids who wore the right clothes and watched the right TV shows and the ones who didn't—and I was firmly on the latter side. Not to Julia, though.

"You lived in Chicago!" she said. "Once my parents took me into Chicago to see the opera and we went to a restaurant where they wanted me to try the oysters and they were really gross, but the opera was the best thing I have seen in my whole life." I'd sure never been to the opera. But it was enough to make her think I was cool, when nobody else did, and just like that we were friends.

And we stayed friends, even though we didn't actually have that much in common, aside from being total nerds and devastatingly unpopular. I went to protests and mathletes competitions, she went to Shakespeare in the Park and the art museum. But we usually went together, even the math competition when we carpooled with this guy who planned to crack every major unsolved problem in mathematics before he got to college, and carried a book of them around so that no one ever forgot he was working on it. Even when Shakespeare in the Park did *Twelfth Night* with finger puppets. We were friends not because we always had things to say to each other but because we could sit beside each other with nothing to say; we understood each other's little gestures and unspoken words.

When we started this year, Julia's skin had totally cleared up and she'd turned out pretty and almost popular, nerd-popular, with a boyfriend and her drama friends. This year I called her more than she called me. This year she cancelled our plans—not often. Just a couple of times. And maybe it was just because everyone was saying we absolutely couldn't screw up junior year if we wanted to get into college, and we didn't seem to have time to breathe between homework and extracurriculars. But maybe not. Maybe she already didn't need me, and she was just waiting for me to notice. But if I thought that, I didn't say anything. I still needed her, as long as she'd keep me around.

I don't know whether she twigged to any of this. When we left Ollie's and got in her car she was still chattering on, with bits of plot, bits of music—"There should definitely be a betrayal in there somewhere—and, like, kotos, and shamisens, and, what else is Japanese?" And then she interrupted herself, stopped short.

"Hey, Cassie?"

"Yeah?"

"Got any plans for summer?"

So deep in winter, summer seemed like nothing so much as an illusion someone had made up to keep us from committing suicide en masse. It was way too early for plans.

"Not really. Going to music camp again?"

She stuck out her tongue. "I've been working double-time all year on one play after another, and if it's not rehearsals, it's voice lessons. Which is fine, but clearly I don't need to go to the middle of nowhere to do more music." She brightened. "Which brings me to my topic. Going to the middle of nowhere just because we can! You, me, here to California. How about it?"

Yes! I said in my head. "Ollie won't perish without your constant presence?"

"He just plays up the angsty pretty-boy thing to get girls."

"Obviously it works."

Julia snickered, and no matter how many times it happened it felt like a surprise, and a relief, when she had a sense of humor about their being attached morning, noon, and night. She was still my Julia, after all.

"Your parents okay with you going that far?"

"My car works okay. I won't be by myself, and it's not like I'll be with a guy. As long as I call home every ten minutes so they know I wasn't carried off by bears, they're okay with it. It's probably the least trouble I could get into this summer." She paused a minute, then glanced at me. "Oh."

"Oh" meant this: When I was happy with them, I considered my parents quirky and supportive. When I wasn't, they were outdated, overprotective fascists. We had rules like no TV in the house until I was twelve, and no cable even then. Like no car for me until I'm eighteen and have the money to pay for it myself, because of global warming and smog and how I have two legs that work just fine. They wanted to shield me from fast food, advertising, and the military-industrial complex. I wondered if there was the slightest chance they would let me take off on my own for a whole summer.

"No harm in asking." I grinned.

I didn't even care that much whether we got a yes or a no; there was something sweet and triumphant in knowing that she would ask me at all. But even if I didn't care that much, there was a lot of begging and pleading and promises to be careful.

In the end, it was a yes. We got photo books out of the library, Route 66: Chicago to Santa Monica. We lay beside each other in her bedroom, pointing at maps, finding landmarks and tourist traps, and checking on the Internet with the same reckless abandon of planning that we'd always thrown at everything we wanted but couldn't have right away—as if getting all the fiddly details to line up would bring the summer on that much sooner.

Then came the May night when my parents woke me up at three, and Ollie picked me up and drove me to school in the pouring rain—the way he and Julia always picked me up so I wouldn't get soaked—and locked himself in the music room for the whole day, and you could hear the wrong notes and the crashing chords on the far side of the hall in my French class. I couldn't play music. I couldn't even speak. I sort of mumbled *"Je ne comprends pas,"* I don't understand, when Madame called on me, and let her pass on to the next person. I didn't understand. Her goneness was too big to hold in my hands, too slippery to grab at.

It was all planned out, which towns we'd stop in for the night if we made good time, and which diners the Internet forums recommended, and which landmarks we could stop at. So the worst that could happen was that we'd get a late start, get lost, blow a tire in the middle of nowhere. This was not in the picture. It was senseless. It was random. She'd been out late, trying to get home by curfew and driving too fast, and the road was dark and twisty and slick with rain. And I wished that it could be someone's fault, but it wasn't. And I didn't let myself think that it was. It was just what happened.

It pressed against my heart until I thought I couldn't breathe anymore.

I don't remember anything about those days. I was sleepwalking and silent. I went to my classes because I couldn't think of anything else to do, made careless mistakes on tests. It was a fuzzy dark limbo in the space between Julia and After Julia, until the memorial drew that bright line to the other side.

I didn't like to go to church. Sundays I went to the Friends meetinghouse with my parents, but that was different. It was small and house-shaped and I knew almost everyone at least well enough to nod and say hi.

Real churches made me nervous; everything was dark, old wood, impossibly solemn. My eyes kept darting around to every corner, as if I expected somebody to be watching me, to realize how out of place I was and how I was doing things wrong.

Last time I'd been there was Christmas, with Julia in

her green velvet dress, singing about the bleak midwinter and angels we have heard on high. And I stared at her until I thought everybody could see me staring, and then I had to turn away, look at every window, at the saints and martyrs and apostles in jewel colors.

Now I tried to match stories to the stained-glass windows, but when I saw the martyr struck through with arrows, the reality of death, and the weight of it all, fell down upon me, and my jaw tensed up all the way to my neck, and the windows dissolved into bright colors and blurred shapes. I laid my hands on the sharp splintery wood of the pew in front of me and put my head on my arms.

Then I felt a hand clamp down over mine and looked up. Jon sat beside me, carefully groomed, bleached tips of his hair dyed back to a soft brown. *He* belonged here, even if he didn't, really. He knew this church.

He leaned in and whispered, "I promised myself I wouldn't set foot in this place again." He quirked his eyebrows, like he might have laughed in other circumstances. "I promised the pastor too."

"That bad?"

"You didn't hear about it?"

I shook my head. "Not the details."

"That's probably for the best. Let's just say it was pretty colorful."

Jon was Julia's very first friend, from Sunday school, and youth group after that, and of course—especially—

choir. He sang with a clear, dark, sweet tenor that stopped people in their tracks and made them listen, and he always got the good solos. It was a voice that made the girls swoon.

He fell in with the drama nerds in ninth grade, right after Julia introduced him around, and it was like she'd given him permission to be someone he wasn't allowed to be. It was like he'd come back from the dead, grinning at random moments and bouncing into rooms. At first I didn't know why.

Jon and Julia dated for three weeks in eighth grade, and then, without much explanation from either Jon or Julia, we were all friends again, and went on as if nothing had happened. She must have known, but he didn't come out to his parents, and to the rest of us, until last year. Nobody was surprised—he was always a little, well, fabulous—and my skin crawled with the wink-and-nod of it all. It just wasn't right to speculate and make assumptions about someone who happened to like musicals and great shoes. People had been making assumptions about me too.

Something happened after he came out, and everything got very tense for a while. It's one of those stories that hangs in the air but never gets discussed, and if you're lucky you'll hear it through the grapevine, but if you're me, then you'll never summon up the courage to ask anyone about it directly. Whether he quit or got kicked out, he was out of the church choir, out of church altogether. He flew his Gay Pride flag high and made lewd comments about Bible study club. There was a weird atmosphere when we went over to his place, like he would spontaneously combust if he stayed around his parents for any longer than absolutely necessary. I could see why. There were actually Precious Moments cross-stitches hanging on the wall. And one in Jon's room, which he had pointedly taken down and laid facing the wall, because "You never know. I might have a person over. Someday."

So yesterday he'd said he wasn't coming to the memorial at all. But here he was. *Oh, because Julia can talk him down from just about anything,* I thought—and I caught myself thinking it, and had to remember again that she wasn't here anymore.

The organ sounded, and feet shuffled. Jon tugged at my arm and I got up, a second after everyone else. The choir started filing to the front, a wave of bright white. I fumbled around in the hymn book, blinking until I could see words again, with Jon's finger pointing me to the right spot. I looked up at him then. I could not remember ever seeing him so hard and determined and sincere.

He took three steps to the left, and he was among them, black suit sticking out, but they parted and rear-ranged themselves to let him in. Had he planned this, is that why he'd dyed his hair and worn a suit? Or was it just a sudden, certain whim? I hoped for a second that it wasn't a prank, but of course it wasn't. He carried himself like one of them, one of the ones who could sing about God without any sarcasm or bitterness showing through. Right now I wouldn't even have trusted myself to do that.

"The king of love my shepherd is, whose goodness faileth never. I nothing lack if I am His, and He is mine forever." I kept my finger on the lines, in the hymn book, not trusting myself to look up at him.

Just the day before he'd sworn off the funeral.

"In death's dark vale I fear no ill with Thee, dear Lord, beside me."

Today I could make out his voice, even in that crowd of twenty or thirty. At first he sang loud, and defiant, his voice ringing high above all the rest.

And then, at the end, even that was gone. It wasn't a protest, a point to make. He just sang.

We came down to the cemetery with flowers a few days later. Didn't go near Julia's headstone, though; we walked long, slow circles around the perimeter, saying almost nothing. Oliver and Jon and Lissa and Amy and me, and I realized again that they all would have been friends with each other anyway, because they all worked on the same plays and saw each other in music theory class, but the only tenuous thread that connected me to any of them was Julia.

"What was that about?" Ollie finally asked, and we all knew what he meant.

Jon shrugged. "I have a bad habit of doing the first thing that pops into my head."

"But it's you," Amy said, exasperated, and we all knew what she meant.

He shrugged again, a studied, elaborate gesture. "Yeah, and it's exhausting being me, sometimes."

"Weren't you scared somebody was going to take it the wrong way?" I asked. "Like it was some political thing, or whatever?"

"What do I care if they think that? It's not like I was singing for them."

He broke off from the path we'd been circling and wended his way among the gravestones. "Julia's the only person who really argued with the pastor on my behalf, and argued with me on his behalf too. Like she was trying to get two of her friends to stop having a stupid fight."

"That's how she was," Lissa said, winding her fingers around thin dark braids. "Remember in tenth grade when our social studies teacher wanted us to pretend that American history was a medley of freedom and rainbows without any complications like genocide? That would've ended in a riot if not for her."

And that was the weird part, wasn't it? I was the pacifist one, at least in theory. But she was the one who actually knew how to cool tempers and smooth rough bits
over and smack people and tell them to grow up when
they needed to hear that. Not me.

Jon shook his head. "I just wanted her to stop it, and
let me be. I thought I was being all bad-ass by refusing
to have anything to do with them."

He knelt down to the ground, by her headstone. Picked
a blade of grass, and peeled it apart, gathering all the
pieces in his hands. That was familiar. When we all used
to sit under the big oak tree to eat lunch, he would shred
the grass obsessively when he was nervous. But this time
he was doing it with such meticulous slowness, as if fighting a losing battle against the habit.

"After they're dead seems like a stupid time to finally
listen to someone, and it seems like everyone keeps trying to tell me what I can feel or can't feel. I'm still trying
to figure out if I believe in God or I don't believe in God
or believe in a God I don't even want anything to do
with, whether I'm even supposed to hope against all the
hope in the world that there's still a place for Julia somewhere. I thought it was that complicated. But it's not. I
just can't not sing for her. I can't."

And where it was just us, away from the nineteenth-
century hymns and the stained glass, they picked up
songs and sang at her grave. Not sad songs, but songs she
liked, songs she'd hum while doing homework or dance

to when they came on MTV. All of us, grass-stained and heartbroken; me, off-key and singing anyway. Because Julia used to tell me to.

We started reassembling our old routines, bit by bit. We started hanging out under the big oak tree for lunch again. And then, one day a week and a half after the memorial, Ollie came up to us holding a huge sheaf of paper in his hands.

"You know how Julia was working on a big secret project?"

"Wait, that was a *real* secret project?" Amy said. "I sort of assumed the secret project was making out with you." And I snickered, even though I shouldn't have snickered, because every so often I would e-mail her or pass her a note inviting her somewhere, and she'd just answer CAN'T, SEKRIT PROJECT. And then I'd assume the same thing.

"Much more exciting than that," Ollie said, and he started passing out his photocopies—thick enough that they were held together with the big industrial-size staples. The first page bore its title in a big typewriter font:

TOTALLY SWEET NINJA DEATH SQUAD

LIBRETTO & SCORE

MUSIC & LYRICS BY JULIA REINHOFFER

P.S. THIS IS NOT A REAL DRAFT, SO STOP
READING, OKAY?

P.P.S. I REALLY MEAN IT. WAIT FOR THE
SECOND DRAFT OR I KILL YOU.

"This is what we're going to do," Ollie said.

NOW

It's intimate, putting on a musical. Like staying with someone else's family. Everyone was working on the same thing (even when they were doing it separately, and in silence), and we were in each other's hair all the time, having tiny arguments about what music to listen to or eating our sandwiches together in the classroom we'd commandeered, or having collective meltdowns at three in the afternoon when everyone was tired and cranky and on their last nerve. I was in the habit of staying out of it, working in the basement, making my own plans on my own time. It felt comfortable that way. But more and more, I tried to push myself upstairs, and eat lunch with the rest of them, and remind myself that these were my friends too. They weren't just putting up with me.

For three years now, they'd been trying out for nearly every play the school put on, throwing themselves into large parts or small parts or no part at all except helping out with the technical bits. This was different. We didn't have a teacher organizing everything and telling us what to do; we just had Ollie, and he wasn't organized enough to tell any of us what to do.

But even though we had less than two weeks to go before school started, and I didn't see how we were ever going to finish on time, somehow we were pulling things together. Oliver was slowly assembling a band out of the school orchestra and the school jazz band. Lissa took over control of the freshninjas from Amy, and for all that she was a short, quiet girl with a hint of a Haitian accent, she knew how to yell when something needed to get done, and intimidated them so much that they settled meekly down to the painting and sweeping and turpentining that she assigned to them.

I'd read enough of the play by now to know about the freshninjas. In the second scene—right after Loud Ninja, Buddhist Ninja, and Flamboyant Ninja, as played by Amy, Lissa, and Jon, sing their song about how great ninjas are—the ninja princess's entire clan gets attacked by the army of a feudal lord. Nearly everyone, in both the army and the ninja clan, dies in an impossibly gory spree of blood spatter, leaving the ninja princess and the three surviving ninjas to seek vengeance. I guess I shouldn't have been surprised that it was easy for Ollie to find forty people who wanted nothing more than to die a suitably bloody and spectacular death onstage.

A few days after Heather drove me to the hardware store, I heard clashing and violence going on somewhere above my head. I crept up the stairs and into the theater, and tried to find an inconspicuous seat at the end of the fifth row. I was still a little frightened of seeing too much of Julia there, and yet . . . I wanted that too; it was really Julia, not some construct that I'd made up in my head. It was weird and silly and dramatic, and I missed that.

They were rehearsing the sword fighting now; no songs there, just panting breaths and the clicking of balsawood sword against balsawood sword. Ollie and Heather, darting close to each other and away again, parrying each other's blows.

Totally Sweet Ninja Death Squad was a pretty conventional story of revenge and doomed love. Ollie was Hiromasa, a samurai who served a powerful daimyo, a feudal lord, while Heather was Himiko, the ninja princess whose family had been killed by the daimyo's army. Obviously, the two of them were destined to fall in love—and we all knew that Julia must have written the part thinking of herself, even if she knew she was a better writer than a singer/actress/sword fighter. And this was the scene where Himiko, vowing to avenge her family, came to murder Hiromasa, managed to catch him alone, and ended up falling in love with his swordsmanship.

She was dressed in a tight-fitting belted black gi, a cartoon picture of a ninja outfit, with a lace trim because she was the princess. Bright white against the darkness. She sank into a crouch, spun out a kick, grabbed at her ankle for a knife and leaped up again; she moved like water. Dark hair floated out around her face, seeming lighter than air for a second. Ollie attacked and she parried, and then drove him back against a wall with a knife at his throat.

"My family is dead because of you."

"They weren't innocents. You know that as well as I do."

"And neither am I. What do I care about innocence in the eyes of a lord who feasts on the taxes of starving peasants? I'll have my revenge."

"Kill me, then," Ollie panted.

And then, taking her knife, she drew it across his face; not to kill him, but to maim him, so that she'd be able to see him for the killer that he was, and not the very pretty man standing a few inches from her face.

"You won't see me coming, the next time I come for you," she whispered dramatically. "You'll jump every time you hear a rat shiver in the darkness. Every time you hear a cicada take off from a leaf. But you'll be dead before you can turn around."

It was just rehearsal. No lighting, no music, no fake

blood on Ollie's cheek. None of the artifice that makes the actors change from the people you eat lunch with to imaginary people from hundreds of years ago. But it made me go wow inside, for how much of Julia I could still see in it, and for everything else. Heather played Himiko as graceful and deadly at once, swift and athletic and—impressive.

I whistled from my seat in the back.

"I am forgiven my casting decision?" Ollie asked.

I raised my hands in surrender. "Well. She does make a pretty good ninja princess."

But it hadn't ever been about that part, had it? It was about loyalty. It was about sticking up for one another. The same time as part of me was thinking about it logically, thinking that they'd been lucky to find anyone who'd make a really good ninja princess, the other part of me was still thinking, Why did it have to be her?

"Whoo-hoo!" she said, grinning as if all that wasn't between us. She brandished her sword and made a few feints at Ollie—then something caught her feet and she tripped, collapsing head over heels.

She started to pick herself up, and she looked at me and just started giggling like a wild thing, and fell over again.

"You show-off." Ollie shook his head and hauled her to her feet. And I tried not to smile. I wished I could pretend like she did that everything was okay. I'd told her I would—told her I'd try, anyway. But I kept seeing her sitting beside me in class, back in eighth grade, and whispering with her friends just loudly enough that I could pick out the contempt in her voice, occasionally smirking in my direction. Or when I was in the middle of telling Julia that my mom was taking me shopping for new clothes over the weekend, and she interrupted all fake-nice how great it was that I was finally getting new clothes, and was I going to Goodwill?

It wasn't as if I stood out. I couldn't wear designer labels, and usually Mom just raised her eyebrows if I picked up something with rhinestones or sequins or anything that she called a ridiculous fad. I wore jeans and T-shirts and didn't care, really, one way or another, but Heather had seized on what she could.

Middle school is like an iceberg, though, everything dangerous under the surface. I heard plenty of rumors and innuendo about me thirdhand, even though she almost never said anything I could confront her directly on, if I'd had the guts to confront her in the first place. But then I'd overheard her teasing Jon—I couldn't even remember now what it was about—and I told her to lay off him. It was right before sixth period, and the halls were packed with people going off to their afternoon classes or squeezing as much social time as possible into the last few minutes of lunch. And she turned right at me and said, loud enough for everyone to hear, "*You* just leave me alone, dyke."

So how did that matter less than whether she could

sing, or look convincing with a balsawood sword? It mattered less because this whole production wasn't about me. I knew that. But that didn't make it easier.

"I took ballet for a little while," Heather explained, down in the workshop. "Had the right sort of figure for it, at first, if not the enthusiasm to keep it up for too long, but it taught me all kinds of things." And she spun around in a loose pirouette as if to make her point. "Overscheduled overworked overachiever. You know the deal."

She always seemed to be down in the workshop with me in the evenings. She'd been put to work on the costumes, finishing off seams and hems, and adding trim; she spent a lot of time with her face bent over her work like some Renaissance maiden doing embroidery, if the Renaissance maiden had neon tights and a skull and crossbones babydoll T-shirt. It wasn't as if I could raise any objections against her sitting there, mostly quiet, changing the CD in the stereo every now and then—but I had to wonder. I tried to "Mmhmm" in a way that suggested I didn't care all that much about what she had to say.

"So, when I decided to transfer, my mom thought I should get involved in some kind of extracurricular over the summer so that I would make a couple friends before school started. Also to give me something better to do than mope and watch reruns of *What Not to*

Wear. And I saw the flyer for *Ninja Death Squad*, and I thought maybe I would be good at that, and maybe it would be fun. I didn't know you were involved, and if I had I wouldn't have even bothered, and then all of a sudden it turned into this big thing—"

"Why are you down here all the time?"

She shrugged. "This is the workshop. I have work to do. *Quot erat demonstrandum.*"

"I guess."

"I don't have anything better to do anyway. The people I thought were my friends aren't. I'm not going to call them up and ask them if they want to check out that cute boutique that just opened up." She sighed. "What you mean is, it's weird, and even if we're technically on speaking terms with each other nothing's really changed and it's not like we're anything close to friends. So why would I stay here?"

"Yeah. I guess that is what I mean." I thought she was half joking when she said that all she wanted was for us to peacefully ignore each other. But that's exactly what we'd been doing for these past few days.

"Because it's never going to get any less weird if I don't," she finally said, carefully.

I chewed at the bottom of my lip. "I don't see that it's going to get any less weird either way, but this CD has been on repeat for the last two and a half hours."

Heather picked up her CD wallet, and when I put down my wood and my sandpaper, she lobbed it at me.

I threw my arms up and it bounced off, and I just managed to catch it before it hit the ground.

I saw some things that I recognized, and some that I
didn't, and toward the end I came to a couple of silver
CD-Rs, marked only with a date. Curious, I flicked open
the CD player and started the music.

Heather stiffened a little in the first couple seconds,
as if she herself didn't know what she was afraid of,
and then as the drum part came in she swore under her
breath. "Jesus."

"What?"

"Nothing," she said, voice lower. She just stalked to
the stereo, changed the CD, and went back to her seat.

"I don't even know what I did wrong, so don't act
like I did it on purpose."

"Forget about it."

And she looked down, her face half an inch from the
blue silk of the kimono she was sewing, where it was
hopeless to try to get a word out of her.

I went back to my own work and didn't look up until
I heard a crunch of metal. Shards spiked out from under her Doc Martens, catching the harsh light. Heather's
chest was rising and falling slowly, in what seemed like
an intense effort to keep everything under control.

"So, the thing is," she said. And instead of telling me
straight off what it was, she stared at me, and looked
down, and stared at me again. I averted my own eyes. The
ceiling was stark, bare, affording me no distractions.

"That's the mix CD that my ex-girlfriend made for me."

I stared at the ground, trying to get my head around this, trying to understand what she'd said.

Her chair clattered as she got up. "Wait," I said, and she sat down again, but I didn't know what I was asking her to wait for. I didn't have anything to say to her.

There was just this blankness. And all these things I couldn't understand about Heather, suddenly starting to make sense.

I looked up at her, and started to try to say something—I wasn't even sure what—and she flinched away.

"Look, I'm a hypocrite, okay? And I've reaped everything I've sown, and to be honest, it sucks, so—whatever you have to say to me, don't think I haven't told it already a dozen times to myself."

At this point I was obligated to say something sensitive and understanding. What I actually said was, "Well, good."

"So are we even, at least? Or, since obviously you'd go all the way to Oklahoma to get away from me, do I have to prove I've filled up my quota of suffering?"

I kept staring at her, not saying anything, mad at myself for crossing a line and mad at her for throwing it back in my face when it didn't come to a tenth of what she'd said to me.

"Let's just forget I said anything," Heather said.

"It wasn't personal. Me going to Oklahoma, I mean."

"Like hell it wasn't."

"Personal would've maybe gotten me as far as Missouri. Yeah, I was mad at you. And I was mad at Ollie for picking you. But after that burned off, the rest of it was me wallowing around in self-pity, waiting for somebody to pat me on the head and tell me I was special and please will I come back?"

I tried to smile at her, willing her to smile back. And when she didn't, I started telling her about the way the sky looks when you roll out of bed half an hour before sunrise and point your bike westward again.

THEN

When Ollie gave me the libretto, I didn't read it. I didn't even glance at it, and that was the beginning of the end. It was too hard to deal with him. He'd been going out with Julia for two years, practically since the beginning of time, and he was miserable. He skipped class and locked himself in the piano room. We tiptoed around him, trying not to say or do anything to set him off. I got the feeling that he couldn't stand me right now, because I couldn't stand him and his my-grief-is-deeper-than-yours when I was just trying to get up every morning and make myself go to school and try to keep my attention on the creepy afterlife stuff in *Hamlet* when the sudden awareness that I couldn't go see Shakespeare in the Park with Julia this year would knock the air out of my lungs.

We still met under the oak tree, passing around sketches of set designs or costume designs, or in the piano room, where Ollie tweaked chords and harmonies and tempos. But we stepped on each other's toes, and Amy and Lissa nearly came to blows about whether a chord should be D major or D minor.

And more and more, I got the feeling that when Ollie said "we," he didn't mean me. He was building a cocoon around the drama people, the ones who were going to turn *Totally Sweet Ninja Death Squad* into a reality, and while they were chattering about their ideas and starting fights, I was sitting on the outside, watching. Julia had been the one link to these people I wasn't even really friends with, but who I liked anyway, who I wanted to like me. Even without her, I wanted to be part of this family, and I just wasn't.

I was drifting by myself.

Before, I'd been starting to make other friends. Once in a while I went over to have lunch with some of the guys I knew from mathletes (even though some of them needed to be reminded about how to talk to a girl, rather than to a girl's chest). I wasn't the complete dork I was in middle school. Or, if I was, Julia's friends had been making me realize what it was like to be part of a whole tribe of dorks, giggling over the same campy movies. Amy would go on about the tiniest plot details of a movie no one had any interest in seeing, and Jon had almost no impulse control, and Lissa would just blink at you in silence if she was angry, and they were all dorks and no one cared. With them, it was okay if I was a dork too. I wasn't disqualified from friendship.

But after she died, I couldn't talk to the mathletes guys about my dead best friend, and I couldn't listen to them talk about how unrealistic the computer hacking was in the latest Keanu Reeves movie.

Even if they didn't want me, I wanted to be with the people who understood that there was suddenly a gaping hole in the universe.

One Thursday night I got a call from Jon.

"We had auditions last weekend," he said, with way too much nervousness in his voice.

"And I wasn't in the way? I know. I don't want to hear it."

"No, you'd much rather hear that than hear what I am going to say. But I couldn't make Oliver do it."

I knew it was going to be bad. He said nothing for a while.

"Hello? You still there?'

"Uh-huh. Um—you remember Heather Galloway?"

How could I forget? "That's kind of a random question."

"I wish. She is—um—she's our new ninja princess."

I finally managed to say, "What?"

"I know, I know, I know. Just—don't blame Oliver too much for it. It's not really his fault."

"It was his decision, right? So how can it not be his fault?"

My stomach was knotting up. I hung up the phone because I couldn't bear to keep talking to him, and I felt guilty as soon as I had done it, but I wouldn't call him back. And all I could do was play hypothetical conversations in my head, over and over, yelling at Oliver for all the things I'd wanted to say since Julia died, but couldn't, because he was having a hard time and we were supposed to be gentle with him, but I was exhausted now from the effort of being gentle with him when he wouldn't be gentle with anybody else.

That afternoon, we went to the piano room, and the topic came around to whether we should leave the lyrics alone in the third verse of one song or work them over a little because Julia had scribbled on the manuscript "Lame, lame, lame, but I'm moving on for now." With everyone, not just Ollie, but Jon and Amy and Lissa too, trying to stake a claim for What Julia Would Have Wanted, as if they knew, as if the main thing driving forward this whole stupid enterprise was the memory of a dead girl. Which it was, I knew. But Julia wasn't this musical, she wasn't just this girl who could think up song parodies at the drop of a hat and tried out for every play. She was more than that.

So I threw my backpack over my shoulder and went for the door, hoping that I'd be able to escape without notice.

No such luck.

"Cass," Oliver called, sounding testy.

"It's gonna get dark, and I don't ride in the dark."

"What do you have headlights for?"

I turned around to face him again, finally done trying. "I think one fatal car accident is just about enough for this year."

He was leaning over me, just barely, and his hand began trembling on the door frame above me.

"I don't see that I belong here anyway," I continued. "If you want to stay here and keep digging up her grave, knock yourselves out."

"Fine. Go."

I wanted to, and I couldn't. I just stayed there paralyzed.

"I don't have anything left." My voice was shaking. "You have this, and you've got each other, and . . ."

I just had Julia, who was gone. And a map and a mix tape, but that dream was dead too, and I didn't even have my license.

"Why did you put Heather in the play?"

"She was good."

"That's all?" It came out as a squeak. "She was *good?*"

"This isn't a popularity contest. It's not about who I think is a decent human being. But she can act, and she can sing, and she's graceful on her feet, and I think this play deserves that much. Julia deserves that much."

"No. She deserves better than this thing where we're at each other's throats and miserable. And do you really think she'd be happy about putting Heather in the play after how horrible she's been—not just to me, to everybody who didn't fit in? Jon, you remember what she was like to you. And Julia too."

Jon looked at the floor. "Yeah," he muttered. "But a constant barrage of low-grade teasing and smirking is sort of the definition of middle school. If it hadn't been her it would've been someone else."

"It was a long time ago anyway," Ollie said. "And if you don't get that, maybe you *should* just go."

Please. No. "Don't shut me out of this."

"You don't get it, do you?" Ollie said. He only took a step toward me, but it made me back away until I was all the way out in the deserted hall. The others were staring at me from behind him. "I'm just saying what everybody knows. You kept leaning on Julia's pity even after the friendship was over, and she let you."

I was stingy-eyed with the shock that he'd actually say it out loud, but I wiped my face with the back of my hand and bit my lip and kept staring up at him.

"Maybe she felt sorry for you because you didn't

have any other friends, and maybe she was flattered by you hanging around like a lovesick puppy, but you can't mistake that for real friendship."

He turned away sharply. "And I'm not flattered that you wanted to fuck my girlfriend."

I took it like a slap, biting the inside of my cheek. One second more and I would've shoved him; but Lissa was already between us. "Time out, time out, time out."

Jon pulled me out down the hallway, and the door slammed shut. I ran, but he ran to keep up with me.

"Why are you the one who's going after me?" I snapped. "Is it like some gay person thing?"

"It's because if I stayed back there with Oliver, I'd have to beat him up."

"Well, okay," I said. "Get on it."

"Cassie, *calm down*." He sighed. "No, never mind. Get pissed off. You've got that right. But he didn't mean it, and you know that."

"Don't apologize for him."

"I'm not!" Jon said. "I'm just saying."

"Well, don't." I brought the back of my hand up against my cheek again and realized that I had stopped crying. This was the story of my life since middle school. I knew how to deal by now.

"I'll kick his ass if he doesn't apologize. Cut him some slack, though, just for now. It's not such a good time for him."

"It's not party time for any of us! I don't see why he gets

more slack than me just because they were having sex."

"You're right," he said, and was quiet.

We were both quiet for several minutes. "You'll kick his ass for me?" I barely managed to smile.

"Maybe not. I could put superglue on him in his sleep, though."

"That works."

I could breathe again. I was not some pathetic friendless creature, if I had Jon.

I pulled myself up onto a table and sat there, swinging my legs in the air. Not calm, not yet, but cooling down.

"Hey," I said, "can I ask you a question I'm pretty sure I don't want to know the answer to?"

"Shoot."

"Was Ollie really, actually . . . jealous? Of us?"

"Kind of," Jon said. "In the sense that he was jealous when he wasn't Julia's first, second, and third priority, yeah. But he wasn't worried about you putting the moves on her."

"Oh?" I said as noncommittally as possible.

He was very slow to answer, and when he finally said something, it was, "Well, um, it's just . . ."

"It's just I wouldn't know how to put the moves on someone if I had a color diagram and an instruction booklet."

Jon grinned at me. "I wouldn't go that far. You're good with color diagrams."

"It's not fair. You keep your hair short and admit to liking math and don't wear makeup—which, by the way, I am not allowed to do—and don't take an interest in fashion—which, by the way, I am also not allowed to do—and you make it to sixteen years old without ever having had a boyfriend, or even getting kissed, and everybody decides that you're a lesbian. Even if Heather Galloway had never told everybody that I was."

"Lissa says that homophobia is a tool the patriarchy uses to scare straight people into gender conformity," he deadpanned.

I blinked.

"Yeah, well, Lissa paints her nails, and wears more skirts than I do."

Still, he didn't ask. He had more sense than that, and maybe he'd been through too much of life to ask what I had been asking myself since I first discovered that everyone had reached that consensus without asking me.

Because, here was the thing. There was not and had never been a single boy who I really found attractive in an I-want-to-take-off-your-pants-now kind of way. Not in school, not among one-hit-wonder boy-bands and movie stars. I listened to other girls fawning over this one or that one and I just didn't get it. But there wasn't a single girl either. So clearly there was something terribly wrong with me, and I was probably only attracted to Mongolians or something. I probably wouldn't even make it to cat lady status when I got old. Guinea pig woman, maybe.

Except there was Julia, and I still had no idea what to think about Julia.

I had never let myself think about that too long, or too deeply. She had Ollie, and she was happy that way, and I was happy that way, and it didn't need to be any more complicated than that. Except that there was a time I wanted to hold her hand, and didn't, because I couldn't risk someone thinking it meant something. I couldn't risk that it might mean something.

Maybe I needed to risk it.

As we sat beside each other in silence, swinging our legs off the same long metal table, I was starting to hatch a plan.

NOW

Things did not magically revert to Okay between Heather and me. There was no Okay to revert to. Even in third grade when I had just moved from the wilds of downtown Chicago, we'd already been standing on separate sides of the divide between the nerds and the popular kids. Which means that she wrinkled her nose at Lissa when she brought plantains and spicy beans and rice for her lunch, and she ignored Amy as being totally beneath her notice, and even when they were assigned to work together on a project, she'd done all the work because, in her words, it wasn't a project about how totally hot the elves in *Lord of the Rings* were.

She obviously wasn't in the same place as she used to be. She never joined in when someone started debating which one of the Birds of Prey was the best, but she didn't roll her eyes. She even sat next to Lissa at lunch and demanded a taste of her okra etouffee. But she listened to music that was too hip for me and picked out her outfits too carefully. She was still over there, somewhere.

But I found that I didn't mind, so much, sitting quietly downstairs with her. We took turns choosing CDs. I was making miniature crossbows and catapults, and figuring out how to hide a full-size sword inside a wall (not to mention all the little throwing stars—I figured out that I could reappropriate the spring-return doohickey inside retractable dog leashes, so that you could pull them right out of the wall and have them fly back toward it again). Meanwhile, Heather was sewing costumes. So she stared at her work and I stared at my work—but when we couldn't stare at our own work anymore, we stared at each other like two scorpions trapped in a mason jar.

"Tell me something," she said as I pulled out the CD that had just finished to pick a different one.

"Something?"

"Something green." Heather brushed back the hair from her face for the hundredth time, hair that fell back again as soon as she bent her head down to her work.

"Green."

"Like something about the trees. Or the grass."

I let my mind fall back to when I was pedaling across the state. "It's not the grass that's green. By June it's already starting to get bleached pale, and then into yellow, and into brown. There are the trees in Missouri—and, oh. There's the Gemini man. You seen that?"

"Don't think so."

"You'd remember. Over in Wilmington—it's not so far, but it's not a place you'd go to if you didn't have some reason to go there. It's this guy who's maybe twenty-five feet high, and he looks kind of like an astronaut. He's dressed in this hideous green jumpsuit, and he's got this welder mask thing on his head, and a rocket in his hands. It is just about the greenest thing I've ever seen. Right in the middle of this nobody town." I brushed some sandpaper over the wood I'd been working at, trying to think of the next thing to say. "I'd been on the road for an hour and a half, and I was thinking, oh, great, just three hundred more of those and I'll be in California, and—why was I doing this anyway? And then I come upon this guy by the road, and I think, fifty years ago, some people thought it would be a good idea to do this. And they did it. And now we have a giant green guy by the roadside. Like a monument to perseverance in the face of absurdity. I don't know why, but it made me think it would be a good idea to keep going."

"Was it?"

If it had been Jon, or even Ollie, I might have been able to come up with a satisfactory answer to that. But they knew. They'd been there too. I just shrugged.

"I don't think I could've done that. Not even for those legs."

I glanced down at my legs, which still bore a scab from where the bike had fallen on me, and some faint scratches from when I'd scraped them through the thorny brush, and which were furry and unshaven, and I didn't say anything. It seemed like it might be a compliment. It seemed like it might be two compliments. But this was Heather, who always said "Can I ask you a question?" or "I'm not saying this to be mean or anything," when she wasn't asking a question, and was saying it to be mean.

"Tell me something quiet."

She smirked, and pointed upstairs. The saxophonist and the bassist were trying out the melody line from "Vengeance Is Mine," not really getting the rhythm right yet, but they certainly were being enthusiastic about it.

I thought for a while, and then I told her: "I don't know if I ever got any quiet. You could wake up at three thirty, four thirty, thinking that you'd be awake before anything else alive, but even then you could hear the cars and the trucks whizzing down the highway, flashing their headlights in your eyes, and you'd dream down-trodden truckers and unfair labor practices, or exhausted families en route from an old home to a hopeful new one. It wasn't the cars that were loud, but my mind that was never ever quiet."

"You weren't scared? Just—out there by the side of the road?"

I thought about all the times I'd been scared, and I didn't have the right words. Not for her. I breathed in, breathed out.

"It's your turn. Tell me something."

"Something what?"

"Something scared."

"Ouch!" Heather said with a dramatic wince. "Well, I guess I had that coming." She got out of the bony chair where she'd been sitting and lay down on the cement, rolling up her dress-in-progress for a pillow. Maybe because the ceiling was the best place to look when there wasn't any safe place for your eyes to go.

Me, I moved on, measuring things out to sixteenths of inches and repeating my measurements. That calmed me. It took me to a world where you could be assured that as long as you followed the directions conscientiously, things would come out all right, and there wasn't any ambiguity about what you were allowed to do and what you weren't allowed to do. That was much more comforting than anything that existed out here in the real world. Finally, I started chiseling out a wedge in the honey-colored wood as Heather started to talk.

"It wasn't a big school, so everybody knew everybody,

and I had some classes with Gianna. We said hi to each other in the halls, but we were more like acquaintances than real friends. By then I was out to my parents and my friends if I thought they could keep a secret—some people, you know, they love you to pieces but they'll tell all your secrets to the *other* people they love to pieces. It was almost starting to be all right. I could accept me, and my parents could accept me, and everyone else could accept me as long as I was inconspicuous and didn't make any waves. I thought that I could just live a nice quiet high school life, no drama, no romance, until I went off to college. It would be so much easier, as long as I kept my stories straight. And—and then suddenly I noticed the way that Gianna smiled at me like she wanted me to give her a pat on the head. And how she'd glance up at me for a second and then glance down again real quick as soon as I even started to meet her gaze. And then I figured out what was going on, and she figured out that I'd figured out, and by that time it was like—when you're in a foreign country, and you bump into someone who speaks English too, and then you find out you grew up in the same hometown. There wasn't even any stopping to think about whether it was a good idea or a bad idea.

"But that's not the point," Heather continued. "The first time I really noticed, we got put on opposite sides of a class debate, and—it wasn't a big deal or anything, we just tried to argue our points passionately. But after class she ran up to me to make sure there weren't any hard feelings. She kept saying please, and I'm sorry, and please, and I'm sorry. And it hit me, how scared of me she was. It made something connect, in my head—because that was exactly how scared I used to be when it came to you."

My concentration slipped, and the chisel slid, across the wood and into my hand, nicking a long scratch across my palm. Blood welled up to the surface. I ran to get the first aid kit, and while I was standing on my toes looking in one of the cupboards, she kept talking. She was looking at me with her eyes wide and her face pale, and she didn't even stop talking. It was as if she didn't trust herself to keep going if she stopped.

"So, I used to have this really hopeless crush on you. And it took me a while to figure that out, and I didn't deal with it well when I was still trying to figure it out, and once I did figure it out I dealt with it worse. I was mad, and I didn't even know who to be mad at, so—"

"I'm supposed to feel sorry for you?"

I poured iodine onto a cotton ball and held it against my hand, willing myself not to flinch against the hard sting. I kept my back turned to Heather, my face turned away.

"You're not supposed to do anything." Her voice rose an octave to a harsh, angry squeak. "If you don't care that's fine, and if you don't understand that's fine, and I guess—I wanted you to know that I know that I was a pretty poor excuse for a human being back then. And I knew it then too, even if I didn't know how to fight my way out of it."

I couldn't bear to look at her; all my anger burst forth in a wave that didn't give me time to think about it. If she was trying to apologize, if she was trying to explain herself, that didn't matter. I couldn't see it through the haze in front of me. "It's not fair. It's not fair for you to take the worst year of my life and turn around and say that I don't even get to have it to myself, it's about you and your own pain, and about making yourself feel better."

"Jesus. I might have figured out a way to make myself feel better that didn't involve telling you way too much about my personal life."

"What do you think I'm going to do? Spread rumors about you?" I did turn to her then. Her face was so still, it might have been etched in glass. "I know what that feels like. I wouldn't wish it on my worst enemy."

"I didn't say any of this accidentally. Give me a break. I've lived for long enough to be very careful about what I say and who I say it to. I do know when to shut up."

And you said it anyway, why?

As a bargaining chip laid out on the table. As a peace offering. Or just to make me feel sorry for her when she didn't deserve it.

She edged up to me and brushed against my arm. "Is your hand okay?"

"Only a flesh wound."

She left me alone while I bandaged it up and tried to think.

"Me?" I finally said. "Out of all the girls in the school—"

"All the girls in the eighth grade."

"Me. Me?"

"It's not as if you're not pretty, you know," Heather said. Her eyes were on me then; bright, and intent, and asking something.

"I never said I wasn't." I didn't think of myself as pretty though. Or ugly either. I didn't think that I could be put on that scale. It's like one of those kōans where the answer only highlights the absurdity of the question. Does a dog have Buddha nature?

"If I say something, will you get mad at me?"

I knew better than to say no.

"No," I said.

"It didn't matter what I said, it didn't matter what rumors I spread or whether I snickered at you in the hallways. Which, like, I really and truly know I shouldn't have done. People would've made some assumptions about you."

"I know."

"The only thing that would've changed, if I'd been nicer to you, is that they'd have made the same assumptions about me. And I wasn't ready for that, I wasn't even ready to admit it to myself. I couldn't have endured it. You, though—you acted as if you didn't care what anybody else thought about you."

"But I did care," I said. "Between the things I wasn't allowed to do, and the things I didn't know how to do, I could never have been inconspicuous and popular like you. I wished I could be, but I didn't see that I had any choice except to stumble forward until I stopped caring. Or looked like I stopped caring."

"I'm not saying it's *right,* you know? And I'm not saying it makes any sense that some people draw lines between musicals or flannel or haircuts and who you want to make out with. God knows if shoe shopping and makeup could ungay a person, I'd have had an easier time of things."

Heather gave me a sideways sort of smile, like we had shared a dozen painful experiences, like we could understand each other. I wanted to run away and yell, We don't share that, we don't understand each other, go back and be the Heather that I thought you were.

But she put her hand gently over the place where I had bandaged my palm, and she said, "I *am* sorry. I wish I could take it all back. But I can't."

I looked at her like if I kept it up for long enough she would say "Just kidding" and smirk at me. No—she looked earnest, with shards of hope in her eyes, and I knew that she'd tried to give me whatever it would take to start to mend things. Her secrets, her past, the things that hurt her when she poked at them.

And I could almost believe her. I had learned a few things by now about weakness and dishonor.

"It's not okay yet."

I don't know why I said *yet*, but it was out there, like a promise that someday that would change.

"I didn't think it would be."

THEN

I counted money, counted days, counted emergencies and possibilities and contingencies, and then somehow I was certain. I was certain, even though I was terrified.

When I came home Dad was in the garage, going through old boxes. I put my bike up on the stand and got out my tool set to adjust the derailleurs. If I was carrying that much weight I'd need to make sure the gears shifted right.

And it gave me something to do while I was making up my mind to say something.

"You remember this?" Dad said softly.

I turned around and saw a piece of green paper, folded in half, printed up into a playbill. The clip art was atrocious, but the spelling wasn't bad, considering.

"That's from when we did the vampire play, in fifth grade." Not an official school play or anything like that, just me and Jon and Julia being silly with some vampire fangs we found at the dollar store after Halloween. But it was the kind of silliness that takes itself seriously enough to put a lot of time and effort into printing up a playbill.

Things used to be a lot simpler.

"We were supposed to go to California," I said. "Me and Julia."

"I was thinking," Dad said. "After your finals are over, we could take a vacation. Go up to New York, maybe. Or Toronto."

"Sounds good," I said, and for a minute it did sound good because he understood that I needed to be somewhere else right now, and he knew better than to suggest California. But I had to say what I was thinking about.

"I thought maybe I might still go to California," I said.

"By yourself?"

"Yeah."

"How?"

"My bike," I said.

Somewhere between cycling to school and to Julia's house and to the grocery store for a snack or a magazine, I fell in love with the wind in my face and the sun on the backs of my hands. On the bike, I was swift and strong, invulnerable. When I wanted to be carried far away from everyone at school, my bike carried me. And when I started to outgrow my pink bike from middle school with the basket and the streamers on it, I wanted a real bike, a grown-up bike.

I'd found it in the racks at the bike store. A touring bike, a twenty-one-speed Bianchi, lighter than a mountain bike and sturdier than a racer. Perfect for going forever. It spent five months on layaway while I saved my allowances and did chores—and then my parents shocked me with it on my fifteenth birthday. I did my first metric century on that bike, all sixty-two miles of it. My first real hundred-mile century too. "It's built for long distances, and bike camping, and I've got it tuned up nice."

Dad didn't say anything for a bit. He kept shuffling through a stack of old papers.

"You sound like you've thought this through."

"For about an hour and a half," I gulped out. "Which is okay, because I still have to finish school and buy supplies, and I have plenty of time to change my mind, but I thought, if it's hopeless I'd better know right now." He was looking at me, worried and skeptical, as I tried to make my case all in a single breath. "I've been bicycle camping before. Even when it was flash flooding and I couldn't make it home in time, even that one time I got lost and didn't get myself turned in the right direction for hours. I'm a good enough bike mechanic to fix just about everything on my bike well enough to get to the next town, and I've got enough saved up for meals and repairs and hotels sometimes if it's raining. And—in the seventies, there was this kid who decided that he was going to sail around the world by himself. And he did. It was in *National Geographic* or something."

He shook his head. "You and Julia. You always had such huge ideas. And even when there wasn't a chance in the world that you could pull it off, you didn't care." He looked at the old dog-eared playbill again before putting it back in the box. "It doesn't always work like that. When you fall, you can fall hard. And there won't be anyone to pick you up, out in the middle of nowhere."

"Do you think I don't know that? Do you think I don't know that I'm going to be changing flat tires in the pouring rain, and subsisting on freeze-dried reconstituted meat-related product, and sleeping in the grass?"

He sighed. "I never wanted to be one of those parents who kept their kids from roaming around the neighborhood unsupervised and figuring things out for themselves. But it was a lot easier to think you could fend for yourself before Julia—"

My first instinct was to pull out all the statistics I knew about safety and fatalities per hour or per mile. But it wouldn't have made any difference.

"I was lying," I said. "When I said I hadn't made up my mind yet. I have. I think that this is what I need to do. It's what I'm supposed to be doing."

Dad pushed his glasses up along his nose and frowned. My parents were Quakers, and beyond being pacifists, and not allowing makeup and cable TV, this was what they believed in. When the Spirit tells you to do something, you had better be listening. Even if it seems crazy, even if it seems dangerous, you had better be prepared to take a step outside what is safe and sane.

I didn't believe that God told some guy, however many thousands of years ago, "Hey, build a ginormous boat in this desert over here." I liked it as a story, though, because it seemed like the kind of thing God ought to say. There were crazy stupid things that needed to get done, or should have gotten done, or turned out to be wonderful when they did get done. And maybe, if God ever did tell people what to do, it was to stick up for these crazy stupid things that no one in their right mind would ever do otherwise.

Things had shifted in the hour and a half I'd been thinking about this. It wasn't just that I didn't want to work on their play, and it wasn't just that I didn't want to have to deal with Heather and Oliver. I imagined the long flat yellow fields out on the road, where the sky is enormous and you feel like you could go on forever, and I wanted that like I wanted air or water. I wanted to be swallowed up in that great expanse of nothingness. I wanted to devote myself to a purpose.

I looked up, and Dad was looking out of the garage,

toward the great expanse of suburb. "I know, okay? Me needing to do this doesn't mean anything. Everything's a matter of life or death to someone whether it's going to the party on Friday or being allowed to stay out past curfew. And just because I think this is different, it doesn't mean it actually is."

Now he looked at me. "But it is different," he said, and he put his hand on my shoulder and I just nodded because I didn't trust myself to say anything without starting to cry.

"Have you talked to your mother?"

I shook my head.

"She was talking to Sheila a few nights ago." Julia's mother. "She was saying that she didn't know what to do with Julia's ashes. She thought that Julia would have wanted to go so much further."

Sure. Her parents were always putting away money for summer camp, or college, or a piano that was halfway in tune, and there wasn't much left over for big vacations. That was why Julia had wanted California, to get as far away as she possibly could, just for once.

"We know how much she meant to you," Dad said. He waited for a moment.

And that was when I dared to let myself hope.

I spent the whole weekend talking to my parents, and Julia's mom, and starting to assemble a list of everything

I would need to do and everything I would need to take with me. I kept telling myself that I could change my mind about leaving. But I already knew that I wouldn't.

And I didn't know how to tell Oliver.

The next day he'd said he was sorry. He brought me sushi from the organic grocery store a few blocks away, and I said that it was all right. But it wasn't. We both knew that.

I didn't come to eat lunch under the oak tree with Oliver and the rest of them anymore. I didn't go to their meetings. I kept my head down, and I did my finals, and I didn't tell any of them that I was leaving until there was no chance of salvaging anything.

Oliver called me the night before I left, when I was out at the grocery store to pick up some dried blueberries to put in with my trail mix, and I never called him back.

I just left.

NOW

The thing that kept bothering me over the weekend was how Heather had declared me to be not not pretty. On the list of things that I was, I could've put urban-planning radical, and cyclist, and good at math and physics, and pacifist and Quaker and a ton of other things, but any word about how I looked would have gone right at the bottom. It was not on my radar. So as I took my usual look in the mirror just to make sure that my hair was straightish and I didn't have anything in my teeth—I frowned and stared at my own eyes. At first I saw what I always saw:

dust-blond hair down somewhere between my ears and my shoulders. A squarish face. Two eyes and a nose approximately where they were supposed to be. But I kept staring, as if to answer that question: What had she seen in me that I didn't see?

Sometimes if you stare at a word for long enough, wondering if you've spelled it right, the word starts looking completely mysterious to you. Like there's something wrong with it. Like it doesn't even mean what you thought it meant.

I had a moment of strangeness like that. I couldn't even tell that it was me there.

That's not me. I'm younger than that. That girl looks strong—that girl looks like she knows what she's doing.

Maybe that was the me that I had become, changing flat tires in the rain, sleeping in culverts and in deserted fields. And then I smiled at myself, really smiled, not a posing-for-a-picture smile. I was this person who was tough and mature and knew what she was doing, even when she had no clue. And I was also not not pretty.

Monday came. I didn't notice Heather's car in the parking lot, but I started working on the big cardboard castle I was building for the last act without paying much attention to that; it was only as the hours passed that it started seeming really strange to me that Heather wasn't there.

I went up from the basement, not really looking for her, but just looking around.

There were people onstage, but it was just Oliver and Lissa, blocking out some of the sword fighting—someone was squealing, but it wasn't from there.

"Hello?" I called out.

Amy ducked her head out from a classroom. "Get in here!"

"What is it?"

She and Jon, spattered in dark red, were standing over a mixing bowl that very nearly looked as if someone had been bleeding into it. "This stuff is great. So much more realistic than ketchup, don't you think?"

"You do look like you've sustained massive head trauma," I admitted.

"It's really good, though," Amy said. She poked at her head wound and licked her finger. "Corn syrup and water and food coloring."

Jon snickered. "That is extremely sophisticated cuisine."

"Everything they serve us in the cafeteria is corn syrup and food coloring, right?"

"Granted. But can we really use anything this sticky? Anyone who gets splattered is going to spend the rest of the play wanting to take a shower in boiling water and dish soap."

"It's what all the zero-budget movies do," Amy said. "I mean, it's not any worse than chocolate syrup, and that's what Hitchcock used."

They were still debating it when I heard stomping on the concrete floor in the hallway. I turned around and saw Heather—and instead of going down the stairs, she came over in our direction.

"You working today?" she asked.

"I was just finishing up."

"Good. Me too." And she started back out the way she'd come in.

"You just got here."

"It was one of those days. I'm in no mood to take on anything sharp."

I didn't get a good look at her until we were back out in the parking lot; her face was flushed with red and her eyes were dark.

"You want to talk about it?"

"No," she said. "I want to . . . Say, you know the little patisserie at Trailwood and Stanley?"

"I don't get out that way much."

"Okay. Obviously you have not lived. C'mon."

"I was once kissed in a motel hallway by a bass player, at three in the morning."

"Impressive, but unconvincing. I'm buying, so get in the car."

THEN

Every day I had a job: thirty or forty miles, or more, or less, depending on the weather and the hills and whether I had slept on lumpy ground the night before. In the evening, I would add up the miles I'd done, and the miles I had left to do, and I could divide out the miles and the days to reassure myself that I was on track and on time. I could reassure myself that I was doing exactly what I was supposed to be doing. And when I got to California, the good fairy would tap me on the shoulder and I'd be free from the ache that lurked over my shoulder and pounced when I stopped at some roadside diner, or sat in my tent at night. The ache that grew up inside my skin and seized hold of my heart so that there wasn't room for anything else—anything else except pedaling, and pedaling, and pedaling.

It was too much aloneness. In the long stretches I'd catch myself talking to my memories of Julia, or the Julia who should have been here with me now. But I liked having my imaginary Julia to talk to. She was better company than the cars that honked at me.

Julia was saying that of course Ollie was completely in the wrong and she was not speaking to him right now. And then I had to revise it, because it wasn't true; she'd have rolled her eyes and smiled in exasperation and said that of course he didn't really mean anything by what he said.

That was how she was when it came to him, ever since the first day of ninth grade when she'd accosted me at lunch squeaking that Oliver—Oliver, the cute guy from drama camp, who looked older than ninth grade and held her hand once when they were roasting marshmallows—was in her drama class, and remembered her name. And she kept me updated on every detail: He'd smiled at her. They both had bit parts in the play. He hung out with her after rehearsal and asked what she was doing on the weekend, in a conversation that meandered without getting anywhere.

"You could ask him out," I said. "I mean, in theory. It's possible."

She pursed her lips and changed the subject. Two days later, he was at our lunch table, and Julia was radiating glee and I was reflecting her glee, soaking up the happiness that bounced off her and everything was right with the world because love had suddenly become a possibility. It had become a thing that could happen to people.

But after a week, we stopped having lunch together every day. Once in a while, she went off with Ollie and left me to my homework, and I . . . didn't have the right to be disappointed. Because I liked him. Because, if he wasn't quite as cute, charming, and funny as Julia claimed, he was pretty close. Because Julia deserved him.

I remembered him being effortlessly charming, holding a spot in line for me when I had to run to the cafeteria from the other end of campus, and splitting the snacks he brought from home into neat thirds, and I thought that I should call him. Should try to work things out. But I made excuses. I didn't know when I'd be able to recharge my phone battery. He was probably busy with the play right now. He didn't need me distracting him.

I'd been on the road for four days when I camped outside of Bloomington, at the side of the road in my compact travel tent. It wasn't worth the money and the hassle to bother with the public campgrounds, though I had those mapped out in case someone called the cops on me; I tried to get far enough away so that I wasn't visible from the road, and hoped for the best. And I sat down with my map and pencil and paper and worked it out, again: 2,337 miles left, and seventy-six days, which gave me thirty-one miles per day. That seemed like such a possible distance—my parents had friends who commuted thirty miles a day, and they had real jobs. So I didn't even get discouraged when I heard raindrops start to plink down on my tent. Even in the rain I could do twenty, and make it up the next day. No problem.

I woke up in the dark, half asleep, my arms soaking in water. I pressed down hard against the ground, just to reassure myself that it was still there under me, and felt the half inch of water pooling at the bottom of my tent. Blinking hard, I started to collect my thoughts. My stuff was safe—the panniers were waterproof—but I needed to get dry and warm. It might be almost summer, but the nights were still cold, and the rain wouldn't do me any good.

I ducked outside of the tent and saw the road running past, the headlights of cars. Rain was pouring down, and as the cars rushed by their tires spun up torrents of rain onto the side of the road, right where the tent was— right up between the walls of the tent and the ground-sheet. And somehow I hadn't even thought about how far I was from the road, or getting up to higher ground. I crawled back inside to pack my sleeping bag and try to make a plan. Bloomington, only a couple of miles away. A motel. I had enough money for that.

The bicycle seat was soaking wet, and in the rain, the fenders weren't much help when my tires flung up water onto the pants I'd gone to sleep in, but I was already so wet nothing would make a difference. I turned on every headlight and taillight I had until I was in full Christmas tree mode, and from then on into the city, there was nothing but a constant stream of whispered prayer to anybody who'd listen, please don't let me be run over please don't let me be run over please don't let me be run over.

I counted eight honks, three blaring horns, and two screaming curses by the time I got to the first motel I could find, and my heart was hammering in my chest, but all I could think was, It's going to be all right now.

"We're full," said the guy behind the counter. He looked like he hadn't slept in a week, or shaved in about that long.

"I don't even need a real room or anything, I just— I'm totally soaked. I'll hang out in the hallway until morning."

I wrung out the bottom edge my T-shirt and let the water puddle onto the floor.

"I'd like to help you out, but there are rules about this kind of thing."

"Dammit." And then: "Sorry. I didn't say that."

A shape I hadn't even noticed rose from the couch.

Skinny guy, long hair, with an instrument case slung on his back.

"You too?" he said.

I shook the water off of my hair and made my way over to the couch, keeping my distance enough that I wasn't dripping on anything.

"I am perfectly fine," I said. It came out sarcastic, though, and then I couldn't help but laugh. "For certain values of fine."

"And two and two is five, for certain values of two," he said, and I smiled again, because what were the odds that a complete stranger would be telling me a math joke?

"You don't have a room either?"

"I do. It's just that there are people in it at the moment who do not need anyone to disturb them." He rolled his eyes dramatically, and I nodded. Yeah, I had some idea of what that was like.

He brightened. "Hey. I do have a hallway. And a bathroom, which has a hair dryer in it and everything. And I must have a spare T-shirt lying around somewhere, so—" He went over to the elevator and took a backward step inside. "Coming?"

"No," I said. "I'm not really that stupid, am I?"

He kept his hand on the door, holding it open. I looked back at the guy at the desk, who just shrugged apathetically as if I was no longer his problem.

I thought of going back out into the storm, where I could skid, or a car could skid, or I could go unnoticed just long enough to wind up spattered on the asphalt. There was no smart or safe thing for me to do. I might as well choose warmth.

"Okay," I said. "Guess I am that stupid."

He gave the room door a couple of halfhearted knocks, then opened it with his key card and herded me into the bathroom, with his hand over my eyes.

"Hey. What exactly—"

"Just stay here a sec."

I was not going to stay here a sec, because the situation was getting weirder by the minute, and I was beginning to think that I'd just as soon take my chances in the rain.

Especially when I heard the moaning. And the squeaking. I made up my mind to wait outside. I glanced over for only a moment at the dimly lit shapes on the bed— then left, and closed the door behind me.

The guy with the guitar case—who no longer had his guitar case—followed after me. "See, yeah, that was kind of traumatic, right?"

"I didn't really see—"

"So, we're on tour, and at least we have enough money for a hotel room now. One hotel room. Doesn't allow for much privacy, but his girlfriend drove all the way up from Ohio to see us play, and—these things happen. Oh—I got you a T-shirt . . ."

"Thanks. Can you let me in so I can change?"

He fumbled at his pockets. "No way. I must've left

the key . . ." He slumped down against the wall. "I'd bang at the door, but it wouldn't do any good."

I took the shirt he was holding and started to mop off my hair. Pointedly looking—at the wall, at the floor, definitely not at me in my really unfortunate wet T-shirt. "You change, I'll go get some sodas. Very far off down the hall."

It was deserted in the hallway, at three in the morning. I turned toward the wall and quickly switched my rain-soaked shirt for the almost dry one, and even though my legs were still wet it felt like crawling under warm sheets on a cold day. The shirt was black and red and much too big for me. It said NUCLEAR SUMMER on it in careful type.

He came back bearing two bottles of soda in one hand and held out his other. "Kris Stott. Nuclear Summer, on bass. You haven't heard of us."

"You're right. Cassandra Meyer, on bike."

"Should I ask?"

"Nah. But—thanks for getting me out of the rain."

"Thought it would make a good story. Which is the best revenge for getting kicked out of my room. And it's not so often that girls in need of rescuing come around."

"What makes you think I need rescuing?"

He shrugged in an elaborate way that suggested he wanted to get out of that particular minefield as quickly as possible.

"Everything I really need is in a waterproof bag, and some changes of clothes too. A little water's not going to kill me. But it sucks, so thanks."

"Do you have anybody you could call?"

I looked down. "I don't need to call anybody."

"If you were on your bike in that storm, something bad could've gone down."

"If I had to . . ." I sighed. "If I had to, I could work something out. But it's far already." And I couldn't even conceive of admitting defeat. Of coming back with my tail between my legs, asking for help. Because it had only been four days, and everything was going just fine.

I grinned. "Besides, it's more interesting if I have to get myself out of the situations I get myself into."

"And I guess being outside in the rain is interesting?"

"That's not the word I'd use," I said. "But this part is."

"Glad to be of some entertainment value, then."

We both turned quiet, sitting in the hallway beside each other with knees and elbows touching. I felt like I could fall asleep right there—with the rainfall against the windows, and the sound of branches whipping themselves in the wind. The air was humid and sticky with a tang of air conditioner, and I nursed little sips of my soda, which was intensely sweet, delicious even though I was still half shivering with cold.

"Normally I'm not allowed to drink soda."

"Are you allowed to run away from home?"

"Not normally. But this is an exception."

Kris looked over at me like there was something I was supposed to do, or say, and I didn't know what it was. "You really don't want to go into details, do you?"

"It's not some horrible family situation or anything. It's just life. I'm dealing."

"By yourself, though."

"There are worse things."

He moved from his place next to me with his back against the wall, out into the hallway at an angle across from me, and reached over to brush the water from my hair, his hand nearly skimming my cheek. I closed my eyes and leaned my head back. All day long I'd been thinking about Julia, and Ollie, and what it had been like when they'd first started dating, and this weird combination of feelings—how happy I was at her happiness, and how much I didn't want her to go away and leave me by myself. How desperately I wanted what she had, and how I didn't know if I really did after all, because she didn't think clearly when it came to him, and how I could somehow just not imagine myself into her place.

And I so wanted to, because it would have been much simpler.

We'd been twelve years old together. We'd shared the convictions that only twelve-year-olds can share, that love is simple and powerful and easy and inevitable. And so much more inevitable when it's three in the morning and you're sheltering from a storm, with my hair still damp, and the rain drumming on the roof, and all of a sudden his hand was on my shoulder—

And he kissed me.

"Oh. Gosh." I dropped my voice to a whisper. "Um."

And then I started grinning to myself, without any thought behind it but a Wow! I have been kissed, for the very first time ever! There is a person somewhere in the world who actually considers me kissable!

"What?" His fingers nestled in the tangles of my damp hair.

"I want to tell all my friends, right now. I want to wake them up in the middle of the night just to say that I have had my first kiss and it was in a motel hallway with a bass player whose T-shirt I was wearing. And I really shouldn't have said that, should I?"

That last part was because he was looking at me all disconcerted. Of course he was, and I could hardly blame him for that. But there was something about being far away from my life and from everyone I knew. I could be anyone and it would never get back to them. And I didn't have to care, and I didn't have to be sensible.

And I realized, almost at the same instant: I wanted to tell Julia. It threatened to knock all the elation out of me, and I chewed on the inside of my mouth to make it stop. I got up and went to the window, which was locked and mosquito-screened so that I couldn't actually lean out of it the way I wanted to, but I looked up toward the corner of the sky that I could see and yelled, "Julia! You saw that, right? You totally saw that!"

I laughed; I laughed, maybe for the first time since she died. Because I had been kissed, and because I was yelling up at no one in the sky like a lunatic, and because I knew or felt or imagined that Julia was right there with me, clapping her fingers together in that happy-excited way she had, and giggling, and swearing to embarrass me by calling everyone she knew.

"I'm not actually insane," I said, turning around. "I mean, I can understand why you might think that and it's all right if you do think that, but I just wanted to say that for the record."

"Lots of people have an imaginary friend . . . I guess," he said, in a certain it-takes-all-kinds voice that said he'd seen stranger things.

"Well, more dead than imaginary."

The door creaked open and someone I assumed to be a band mate stumbled out, dressed only in boxer shorts. "Anybody want to explain what's going on?"

"Got locked out," said Kris. "I was a little too eager not to see you having sex." He bowed slightly to me. "Your shower awaits."

"Oh, I—I'm okay." I felt intensely awkward. Like I wanted to get out of here fast before I had to poke at any more sensitive places. "Let me just camp outside your room tonight, and I'll give you your shirt back in the morning."

He shrugged. "You can give it back next time you go see us play."

NOW

The bakery was decorated in crayon-bright colors that almost reassured you that nothing bad could ever happen. We got a small, high table by the window and ordered cakes that were tiny and perfect, layered with chocolate and fruit.

"Of course I had to be dumb enough to pick the place I always used to go with Gianna. But I'm not going to think about that now."

"It's out of the way." And also, as far as I could tell, out of the way from St. Joseph's, and from Heather's place.

"That is the point." She raised her eyebrow and stuck her fork into three layers of chocolate mousse. "She used to get antsy when we sat by the window . . ."

"You didn't want to talk about it."

"I lied. And plied you with pastry."

She smirked, and I smiled back, a little befuddled. I was okay with us being civil to each other. I was okay with us talking through our issues. But since when were we *friends*?

But I got the sense that this wasn't the right time to argue with her. So I didn't. "You can do that, if the food's this good."

"So. Last night my sister and brother and nephews came over for supper, and while I was sprawled out on the floor in the middle of playing knights-and-dragon with the little guys, there's a knock at the door and it's Gianna. And we have a great big screaming fight right out there on the porch. And all I can think is—for months I wished that I could introduce her to my sister and brother and little nephews, and *that's* how it finally happens.

"Karma," Heather said, pointing her fork at me. "You see? The universe has dealt with me for everything I did to you."

I didn't see.

"I spent a good year or two being a total bitch because I didn't want anyone to find out that I was gay, including myself, and by the time I managed to deal with my issues and get myself a girlfriend . . . she was the one who could absolutely not deal with the remotest possibility of anyone finding out. I mean, we both wanted to keep things secret. I didn't want to get suspended, I wanted to stay on the nuns' good side, I wanted to keep my friends. But if we'd been found out, I'd have survived. Eventually the dust would have settled and I'd have picked myself up. Not Gianna. Her family's so conservative that she isn't even allowed to kiss a *boy* until she's practically married, and she really and truly bought into it. She'd have a crisis of conscience and break up with me on Monday, and by Thursday we'd be back together again. So we kissed in supply closets and passed notes to each other in really terrible Latin, or ciphers, and . . . that kind of secrecy was fun for about twenty minutes."

Heather laughed sadly, her head bent low, black hair hanging down the sides of her face.

"I loved her, I did. And when I realized that I loved her, I also knew that I didn't really have a girlfriend. I had a fantasy of what having a girlfriend might be. It wasn't ever going to be real. I was never going to bring her over and introduce her to my little nephews, and I was never going to be able to call her at midnight because I needed to hear her voice, and we weren't going to fix up a cute old Victorian house together and keep iguanas."

"Iguanas."

"I'm allergic to furry things. Besides, they're cute in a sort of ugly way. Anyway. After long enough—after I'd lost my best friend because I was keeping too many secrets from her—it was all too heavy and everything fell apart. Her being scared and guilty all the time, me being mad that I couldn't have more than what we had. We were bound to get caught eventually, and then it would be my fault that I'd ruined her life. And then, well, things got worse, and just when I thought I was okay, I'm not." She snorted, seeming exasperated with herself. "Tell me about Oklahoma."

"Oklahoma?"

"I've never been. God willing, I'll probably never have any reason to go. So tell me."

"Oklahoma was hard," I said. I didn't want to say any more. But she had given me so much. Opened up to me more than I wanted, offered more than I could carry. I searched for something I could give in return, something safe and worthless, and there wasn't anything. "I had my first beer and my first girlfriend and my first breakup, and then I had Oklahoma."

"Oh," she said.

I could see her trying very hard not to look surprised.

When the waitress came by with the bill, she glanced over at Heather. "You bring all your girlfriends here?"

"Only the pretty ones," she answered without skipping a beat—and I couldn't figure out what to say. In the end we went and sat on the bench outside, crisscrosses of wrought iron under my legs, hot from the sun.

"Got my schedule in the mail on Friday. Have you looked at yours yet?"

"Just glanced. But I've got Vesper for English." I stuck out my tongue. "First class of the day."

"Hey, me too!" Her face lit up, for some reason I couldn't fathom. (She did know we were supposed to be enemies, right?) "What've you heard about Vesper?"

"I heard he gave a student negative three on an essay once."

"Out of six? Like an AP exam?"

"Out of a hundred."

Heather sucked in a breath. "Well, you know what? Not gonna worry about it. Because that is the least of my worries."

"So what's the most?"

She raised her hand as if she were about to tick off a monumental list on her fingers, and then she put it down again. "I wish that I could start with a blank slate. I wish I could waltz in there with a fake name and stubbornly insist that I didn't have a clue who this Heather Galloway person might be."

"Is that why you went to St. Joseph's?" The question popped out of me before I'd had time to think about it.

She nodded. "I guess I was trying to get a blank slate with myself. I might've been dumb, but I wasn't so dumb that I didn't notice what a bitch I was. I thought maybe . . . I had some vague idea that I would figure out how to sublimate all my passion into, you know, being a clarinetist or something. Or something would change, somehow, and I'd know what I was supposed to do. Maybe it even worked."

I thought about that.

"Maybe that's karma. Maybe it's not the universe trying to punish you in appropriate ways for everything you've ever done wrong—it's just that you carry with you who you've been and what you've done. And that's enough justice."

That's when I made up my mind.

I decided that Heather would have a blank slate with me.

Maybe it was because she'd been through enough, and maybe it was because I was less and less able to reconcile the girl sitting beside me on the bench with the one who'd teased me and glared at me and made pointed comments behind my back.

I didn't think I could find the words to say it. I wasn't even sure that I wanted to try. But that was okay.

"Look," I said. "I don't want to tell you that things will be okay, because I can't know that. But I think, mostly, people can look back at what happened before and think that we're all just piranhas who had the bad luck to get dumped in the same fish tank, and it's kind of sad but—not the kind of thing you can really get mad at someone for. Not forever."

"Oh," Heather said. She let it hang in the air for a while. "Really?"

"And I'm going to say this even though you'll be popular before the first week's over, and I'm not exactly the person you'd want on your side. But if you need someone to stick up for you, I'll do it."

She was smiling at me like I'd just turned the sun back on. "You are exactly the person I want on my side."

"Lunch," I said abruptly. "If you go out the cafeteria doors and go left, there's a big oak tree not too far away. You should come eat lunch with us if the weather's decent."

"Lunch it is, then," she said with a faint sigh. "I'm not going to be popular, you know. Even if people have forgotten all about me being the mean girl. It's not going to happen."

"But you're one of them." Rich enough, pretty enough, self-confident enough, charming even when she was being mean, as long as you weren't the target.

She frowned. "I don't think I can play that game anymore. Which sucks, because I was *good* at it."

Heather looked at me oddly, her head titled to one side. "What changed? With you and me, I mean?"

"No matter how much I wish you'd just make it simple, for some reason you keep acting like an actual human being."

"At last, all those drama classes pay off." Before she left, she glanced back at me. "I'll give you a ride if the weather's not decent, okay?"

"Definitely okay."

She was the same person she'd always been. Sharp and sarcastic and happy to show off when she was right. And—not the same person. But it didn't bother me as much as it used to.

THEN

When I found a guitar pick, blue and orange with a skull on it, in the pocket of Kris's shirt, the first thing I thought was that I needed to show Julia. And that's how I started my collection for Julia: everything I wanted her to see, everything I wanted to tell her. Everything that I could fit in a small Tupperware box like the one that held her ashes.

In McLean, I found three cat's-eye marbles at the side of the road, their glass surfaces just slightly chipped, and I remembered how Julia had brought all of her eight-year-old's wrath on the boy I lost my marbles to in the schoolyard. And remembered how I loved my cat's-eyes, how they looked like they had an entire universe twisted up inside them, blue and green and orange. In Atlanta—the Atlanta in Illinois, a tiny town where the water tower had a happy face painted on it—a red Hot Wheels convertible. Everywhere, dried grass and corn husks and flowers, forming a soft pad for the other things that I found; and even a hawk feather on a hot day with the sky a stark and too-bright blue.

It was the kind of day that bleached out my thoughts to a dull, relentless, one-foot-in-front-of-the-other determination to keep going for the rest of these 2,264 miles. With seventy-four days left, that made for just over thirty miles a day. I'd lost half a day in Springfield to laundry, and charging my phone at the Laundromat—I could work it out that precisely and still manage to forget that sometimes I needed to wash clothes, sometimes I needed to stop for groceries, sometimes I managed to take a detour trying to find a library and check my e-mail—but I could make it up today if I tried hard enough. It had rained in short soaking storms that did nothing to cool the air; they only made it wetter, like steam coming off a hot iron. I was aware of the heat, and sweat beading against my back and on my forehead, and almost nothing else. The road was so quiet that I let myself drift out toward the middle of the lane, where I didn't have to worry about the crumbling pavement and the bits of sand.

Then a horn blared behind me. I steered right, hugging

the edge of the road where the shoulder fell off into mud and grass. But it blared again, loud and long, and I blinked in panic and frustration, trying to figure out something, anything, to do—I couldn't seem to get it through my head that I should pull over to let the car pass. Before I could think there was blankness, and the screech of the horn, and a rush of smoke and hot wind alongside me, and a voice yelling out "Asshole!"—and me on the sizzling asphalt, my bike toppled over on me.

The following car slammed on its brakes and screeched to a halt a few feet behind me. I looked up, a little dazed, and dragged my bike out of the roadway, into the waves of sharp tall grass. I lay down there—the grass came up as high as my chest, hiding me almost completely. My palms were scratched with blood where they hit the pavement, and blood dripped on the top of my hand too. Experimentally, I prodded my face, and felt something wet and warm against my lip. But I was okay. I would live.

For a while I just lay there and watched my chest rising and falling. My heart was thrumming like a tiny bird, and right down to my toes, my muscles tensed and twitched.

I was okay. I would live.

I told myself that a few more times, and I tried moving my hands and feet just to prove that it was true. But my nerves jangled. I tried to get up and my legs felt swimmy under me.

I could have died. And it was my fault. Half my fault. I wasn't paying attention. I was being an idiot. Even if some redneck decided it would be hilarious to buzz the bike-riding hippie, most bike-riding hippies would've had the presence of mind to get his license plate, and return the insult.

But mostly what was going around my head was just simply, I could have died. Or I could've gotten hurt, bad, and I'd have been left hurt and alone and scared and waiting to die.

Like Julia.

Oh.

I rolled over onto my stomach and leaned my head against crossed arms.

When I stopped at a diner, when I stopped at a convenience store, someone would eventually ask me if I was insane, or if my parents were insane, and if I had any idea how dangerous it was and any number of terrible things could happen to me.

I didn't care. I always said that I didn't care. And now I felt cold all through, to realize that I didn't care after all.

I didn't care because it would be okay if I died.

Of course it wasn't okay. But the idea that maybe it was scared me out of my mind, worse than getting buzzed and landing bruised and scraped onto a country highway. Like the moment when you realize there are real bullets in the toy gun you've been playing with.

It wouldn't be a decision. It would be a split second of

inattention that let my wheel slip into a groove or slam my front brake too hard going downhill, and that would be enough. The tiny part of me that didn't care if I lived or died might let it happen.

I couldn't trust my own head anymore.

After a while I managed to get up, get to my bike and check it for bent wheels and flat tires. I swung my leg over the top tube and glanced back at the road behind me, one foot hovering over the right pedal—and I stopped breathing. I seized up; my throat felt dry. By the time I got off and sat in the grass again, I was trembling.

For the rest of that day and that night, I sat there eating PowerBars and stared down my death.

NOW

I was testing out my miniature catapults. I had two, both the length of my forearm, just large enough to heave a Beanie Baby at someone. I aimed one carefully, at a corner of the workshop, and sprang a purple bean creature into the air.

Heather snapped her head up when she heard the sound. "Oooh. Can I try? Is it dangerous?"

I considered this. "Well, I wouldn't point it at someone's eye or anything. Go ahead, give it a whirl."

She snapped up the other weapon, along with a penguin and a shark for ammunition, and skulked off into the corners that were piled high with costumes and props for ancient productions. It was too small a room to have anywhere to hide, but that didn't stop Heather from flattening herself against the boxes and looking backward and forward like a parody of a spy movie. And then she fired her penguin, just over my head.

"Hey! I *gave* you that one!"

"Then return fire!"

I hesitated. But, well—it was just stuffed animals. Small stuffed animals. That does not even count as violence. So I lobbed a green teddy bear at her, and it bounced off her shoulder.

"I aimed to miss!" Heather protested.

"Too bad!"

And then we were chasing each other around the workshop, not bothering with setting and aiming our weapons, but just throwing the little beanbags at each other, giggling when we could breathe enough to do it. As innocent as two six-year olds in a water-gun fight. We scrambled over boxes and leaped over bits of props strewn on the floor.

Until my feet tripped over something, and I went down on the concrete, tumbling into the space between two towers of cardboard boxes.

It wasn't a bad fall. It knocked the wind out of me, and I could feel a little ache in my hip where I'd fallen, but nothing broken, nothing even bruised.

Heather ran up and leaned over me. "Are you okay? I'm sorry, I didn't mean to—"

"I'm fine, I'm fine, I'm fine." My hands weren't even scuffed.

"Are you sure?" She kneeled down and stretched out her hand. I took a deep breath, and not from running around or falling down. She looked tender and worried, and she brushed her hair back behind her ears so that I could see her eyes, and I thought—Give me a minute. Let me stay here and watch you.

I smiled. "I am one hundred percent unhurt." I took her hand and gathered myself up. And I threw my last leopard at her just to make her laugh.

We didn't see Oliver until he was already down the stairs and in the middle of the floor, his face ashen.

"We have a problem," he said.

We both got quiet real fast. We had a problem, sure, we always had problems. But Oliver looked so serious.

"There's no good way to say this. C'mon, upstairs."

We sat down beside each other on the ugly paisley couch. It was just the three of us—Jon and Amy had gone back-to-school shopping, and Lissa was off at the fabric store's Labor Day sale for the last-minute costume bits she was working on.

Ollie played with his cell phone for an anxious moment. "So we got permission a while back from the principal and the vice principal to put on *Ninja Death Squad,* right?"

"That's what you said."

"Look—I'm not that much of an idiot. I let the principal read the script before school even let out last year, I let him know that it's a play with some blood spurting everywhere, and it has ninja and death in the title, and he seemed to get that it was cartoon violence as opposed to the kind of thing that might be really objectionable. I asked way back a few months ago so that we would have time enough to put together a plan B. So guess what happened?"

I could see where this was going. "He got nervous."

"Not him. But all the flyers plastered up everywhere that say *Totally Sweet Ninja Death Squad*? From what he says, half the parents and all of the PTA are calling up outraged. And they threatened to call the superintendent down on us, and the school board, and the TV news, so . . . he went back on his word. We don't get to use the auditorium."

Heather swore—with astonishing creativity—and coughed, not quite embarrassed.

"What did they teach you in Catholic school?" I teased.

"That."

Heather glanced up at Oliver, who was gazing at us with a look that was so familiar. *You two have a private joke and I'm on the outside.* It was strange to be on the inside for once, special and awkward at the same time. "So what's our next move?"

"What next move?" He slouched back. "We do not have

a stage. If we did have a stage, there's no way two weeks would be enough time to set up for the changes we'd have to make and promote the new location and—everything else that still had to get done in the next two weeks anyway, and that we didn't even have enough time to do."

"We've got a stage here."

"And the community theater people have been nice enough to let us rehearse here, in the hours when it's empty, but they still consider us just a bunch of random high school kids. I talked to them when we were just getting started, and—it was a no. A definite no."

"Well, then, we'll figure out something else." Heather was leaning forward, eyes sharp, her voice rising.

Ollie pressed his fingers against his temples, chestnut hair falling in front of his eyes.

"There's nothing else left to figure out. We're . . . we're not going to make this work. We might as well just give up."

He'd decided that already, I realized. None of the rest of us were even a part of this decision.

"You put in a hell of a lot of work, and I put in a hell of a lot of work. And Amy and Lissa and Jon and—that guy I don't even know who always shows up in his ninja costume, and—just like that, it's over? How the hell can it be over?"

"I know, Heather, I know, so can you shut up about it?"

"And what about Cass? I mean, shouldn't she have some kind of say in this?"

Suddenly they were both looking at me.

And I didn't know what to say.

"Not really," I said. "I'm not one of the drama people."

"You're one of *our* people," Oliver said. "Get used to it."

I thought I could understand Oliver. I could understand what it felt like to be sick of banging your head against things, sick of knocking at a door that wasn't going to open, sick of letting your hopes rise and setting yourself up for another heartbreak. I recognized the exhaustion in Ollie's heart. I'd been there, in Oklahoma. There's a time for giving up.

But there was Heather, as much of a hopeless over-achiever as I was, and angry at her ex-girlfriend for not trying hard enough. Angry at herself for not trying hard enough. I loved her, in that instant, for being completely unwilling to let us not try hard enough.

"It's too soon to give up," I said. "Sleep on it, let us take over. See what it looks like tomorrow. I broke one promise to Julia this summer, and I'll be damned if I break another."

He threw up a hand. "Do what you want to do."

I called up Amy, because she never deleted a single e-mail that wasn't spam, and she had everyone's numbers and e-mail addresses. She stormed in a half hour later with two bottles of Mountain Dew, stuffed shopping bags, her laptop wedged under her arm, Jon following behind her.

"This is not fair," she announced, like we didn't

111

already know that. "As if *Hamlet* and *Macbeth* aren't full of bloodshed! And besides, none of these PTA people ever came to a school play here, and they wouldn't have come to this one, and what's it their business if the front row gets splashed with corn syrup."

We took turns calling people. Everyone. Anyone who might have even the slightest link to an answer. I called the guy who did Shakespeare in the Park with Julia last year, the tiny Asian woman in charge of the giant puppet protest theater, who wasn't really happy that we were producing a completely silly and ahistorical play about ninjas. I ended up apologizing to her a lot.

Then Heather lifted up her head, blinking.

"Why are we making the assumption that we need to ask permission?"

"Um, because we don't own our own theater?"

"Yeah, so we need permission to put on a play. We don't need permission to put on *Totally Sweet Ninja Death Squad*. As long as we can get permission to put on, I don't know, *Rosencrantz and Guildenstern are Dead . . .*"

"*Rosencrantz and Guildenstern are Zombies*," Jon volunteered.

"And nobody would have to know."

"Until the premiere."

"And what are they going to do, haul us off the stage? Didn't anyone ever teach you that it's easier to ask forgiveness than permission?" Heather put a hand on her hip, daring us to chicken out.

Jon was grinning, just out of a corner of his mouth. "I don't know. There is no possible way that we are going to keep this a secret. For one thing, Mr. Vaichon is going to be putting on *Our Town* in the fall, and we're getting started as soon as school starts."

"People have been keeping better secrets than this from their high schools since before we were born," Heather insisted. "Mr. Vaichon—drama teacher?"

"Yeah."

"What's he like?"

"He gets worked up about people who think Shakespeare didn't write his own plays, and he doesn't let anyone get away with slacking, but he's an okay guy." Jon shrugged. "He liked Julia a lot."

"Perfect," Heather said. "Everybody meet me after school on Tuesday. We're going to volunteer for *Our Town*. Vaichon covers for us, we convince the freshninjas to volunteer too so no one tells on us, and we take down our flyers and whisper to people that they should show up anyway."

It wasn't a complete plan. We were still going to have to wait until Tuesday to see Mr. Vaichon and figure out if we had a chance. But it was hope, and that's more than we had a few minutes ago.

I clinked my soda bottle against hers, after we were by ourselves again. "Heather?"

"Yeah?"

"You're kind of a genius."

She grinned. "Come on. For years I lived with *It's easier to ask forgiveness than permission* and *What they don't know can't hurt them* and *It's only wrong if you get caught*. Being undercover isn't always wrong. That's what being a ninja is all about—you're not just being stealthy because it's totally sweet, it's so that you can stay alive. So if our little play needs to go in the closet, bring it on."

That is when I decided something. Or realized something.

I had an itty-bitty little crush.

THEN

I spent hours lying on the grass, one arm pillowed behind my head and the other shading my eyes from the sun, trying to convince myself to get up. My skin began to crawl with twitchy boredom and scratchy heat. I got up and I paced and I sat down again and ripped tufts of grass out of the ground Jon-style, and drank tiny sips of water as if I was in danger of running out. My phone rang, and I jumped. Oliver on the caller ID, and I kept staring at it, thinking that I wanted somebody to say something kind and encouraging to me, somebody I could complain to. But not him. He wouldn't understand, and I wouldn't be helpless in front of Oliver. So I let it ring until it went to voicemail, and after a few minutes I checked the voicemail.

He hadn't left a message.

Even now, almost twenty hours later, I kept hearing the honk of that horn, kept feeling that twinge of my hip and my arm hitting the pavement and the bike sliding out from under me. And I didn't want to, but I couldn't help thinking about Julia, singing along to the radio or tapping her fingers on the steering wheel as she tried out melodies, and then—startled, panicking, realizing that things were going wrong, that she was going too fast and the road was too wet.

It wasn't Oliver's fault, I told myself. I had been telling myself that for months and months and I never made myself completely believe it. She was over at his house, late, and that never happened on school nights—but she had her secret project, and he was feeling neglected, and she made an exception.

She lost track of time. By the time she realized how late it was, it was pushing impossible for her to get home by curfew, but she decided to chance it. Even though it was pouring rain outside, and pitch-black.

It was not Oliver's fault.

He told me all of this, when he felt guilty, and I didn't need to know any of it. I didn't want to know any of it. And I couldn't do anything about his guilt, not when I was thinking, in my worst moments, if it hadn't been for him . . .

I'd been having a lot of worst moments.

But I managed to keep telling myself it wasn't fair to blame him over and over, though I couldn't make myself believe it, until I told him that I was leaving. Until I was standing in front of him clutching that Tupperware urn like he might rip it out of my hands. And everything I said was wrong, and he jumped on every wrong thing I said, and I could hear the words hovering on my tongue. *I'm not the one who said Julia should blow off her homework and come over. I'm not the one who let her go out into that kind of weather at midnight.*

"Do you really think you've been as good a friend to Julia as I have?" I snapped, and Oliver just stared at me. Like he'd heard everything that I was thinking and trying so hard not to say out loud. Well, he'd said his piece to me, and now it was my turn.

He shook his head slowly. "How could I even expect you to understand?"

I guess he was right. I guess I didn't want to understand. And no matter how much time passed that day, no matter how far away I was here at the place on the side of the road where I could blame no one but myself, I could still see his number on the screen of my phone and think nothing except for this: that I didn't want to understand.

NOW

It was my turn to make dinner the night we almost lost our stage and Heather hatched her brilliant plan, so I used it as an excuse to leave before I could think any more about my crazy new feelings. There was a fantastic swooping downhill on the way to my house, and I loved the way I would sail down at twenty-five or thirty miles an hour with a shriek and a squeal. After that, two and a half miles of hills that rolled up and down—a just-right kind of distance. Two and a half miles was almost enough time to turn things over in my head, so that I could come up with an alternative to acting as if I'd just been hit over the head with something heavy.

But twenty-five minutes later, I realized that I wasn't used to the idea at all. There was just a kind of dazed blankness where my brain generally purported to be.

Wow.

So. That's interesting.

I pondered the way I would wait to hear her shoes on the stairs in the mornings. How I used to listen with a mix of guilt and anxiety and dread, and now—I was a little disappointed if she waited too long to show up. And she always came halfway down the stairs to wave hi to me even if she was spending the whole day rehearsing. And if I came up to sit in the audience for a few minutes and watch, she always hammed it up.

She liked me, once upon a time, before I'd been remotely able to think that was even possible.

When had that stopped seeming embarrassing, a convenient excuse to disarm me so I couldn't fight back?

No. I had a better, simpler question than that. Do I say anything?

Are you insane? I answered to myself in the next moment. First of all, drama, by definition, already has enough drama. This, Julia had explained, was why you shouldn't date people when you were doing a play with them. "I mean, it's not like anyone listens to that," she'd said. "Everybody dates everybody anyway, because you're together all the time, and you're pretending to be in love with each other, and it's kind of intense. But you shouldn't. So it's actually a good thing that Oliver hasn't asked me out yet, even though he's really hot, and really nice, because it would just be too much drama." That was, of course, right *before* she asked him out. It seemed like forever ago that I was too young to realize why she wouldn't listen to her own advice.

I liked things the way they were. The past days had been peaceful and calm and happy, working in silence, listening to Heather's CD collection, and talking about safe topics. School. Movies, until she got exasperated with the way I always answered "Haven't seen it" when she mentioned one, and asked me if I lived under a rock.

"It's a very nice rock, I'll have you know, and you should come visit sometime."

It should have been like in fourth grade, when the movies I wasn't allowed to see made me the weird one, the target for jokes, but it wasn't. Because of Heather, who laughed about it and took seriously the pleasures of terrible movies—but also because of me, because I had become more than the things I couldn't do. Because, maybe, I was starting to understand something of peace, and something of integrity, that went further than arguing about whether *Star Wars* counted as a war movie.

Things were like that. Things were good. And she had had a very unpleasant breakup not too long ago.

And, and, and.

I moved through the routine of putting a pot of water

on the stove to boil, and taking the bag of vegetables out of the freezer to thaw a bit, and kept worrying at it like a loose tooth—one minute resolving not to think about it because thinking the same things over and over and over wasn't going to help, and then the next minute coming back to it anyway, because it was there. Until my mother said sharply, "Cassie, that's about to boil over." And I remembered that I was in the middle of something, and put the pasta in the water, and the vegetables in a saucepan. I felt awkward all of a sudden, trying to figure out how to patch up the silence. In the weeks since I'd come back the air was full of all the things my parents and I weren't saying to each other, and I wasn't sure if I ever really expected that I could leave and come back and pretend that nothing had changed, but I wanted that anyway.

"Mom," I said. "The PTA is upset that we're doing a musical about ninjas. I don't think they're gonna shut us down, but they came pretty close." And maybe I hadn't let myself think about that too much, because—since I'd come back, at least—I could make all the excuses I wanted about fictional violence, but I couldn't think about *not* being a part of this thing that had so much of Julia's heart in it.

Sometimes you don't have a choice. Sometimes you just know what you're going to do, past all possibility of being convinced otherwise.

But still, I had to ask. I didn't want to figure things out for myself. I just wanted to hear that I was all right, and not think about anything that had anything to do with Heather. "Do you think it's okay? That it's kind of violent?"

Mom frowned. "When your friend Amy was over here with you and Julia to work on a project last year, she was talking to you about a movie where the killer had blades coming out of his shoes."

"I never actually saw that movie," I said. I felt that I had to add this just for the record, because the blades in the shoes were the least objectionable part in it.

"It made me wonder, I'll say that. I thought I'd raised you better than that. But twenty minutes later, I wander past the kitchen again and you're mumbling that you shouldn't talk about beating the other mathlete team to a bloody pulp, even if it's just a joke. I can't say I understand it, and don't you even think about asking to play one of those Grand Theft games, but—if you're clear on the difference between fictional violence and the real thing, there are worse things."

I drained the pasta and started mixing in the butter and vegetables while Mom set the table. "It's not like it's glorifying violence," I said. "Not really. There's even a song called 'The Flavor of Blood Is Sadness.'"

"And why is the PTA more concerned about high school students pretending to be ninjas and kill each other than the military recruiting high school students to actually kill each other? I would like to know that."

Mom could give a good rant on the military-industrial complex anytime, and I did not mind listening to her rant, because it felt like we were back in our old routines.

And it meant that I didn't have to think too much about anything I didn't want to think about.

semicircles of plastic orange high-school-cafeteria chairs, acutely conscious of my beaten-up sneakers, and my scruffy scratched legs, and my sticky sweat, and my oily hair, and my smell.

I missed Julia.

I didn't know what reminded me of her, but it was there, like something lodged in my throat. She was always there to shove me forward and tell me not to be scared. I needed that now.

I looked around, to distract myself. At a pair of middle-aged men who'd come in together and who moved together with the easy, comfortable habits of old married couples. At a mother with a little infant, swaddled in tie-die and nursing. Embarrassed, I averted my eyes—but I let out the breath I'd been holding. I was not the only one here who was hungry and sticky and smelly and out of place. I felt like I was going to be okay.

I did not feel relieved about the singing. Because I cannot sing. I can just barely carry a tune in a bucket, when it can't be avoided, but I cannot sing.

And I remembered Julia telling me that it takes a lot of courage to sing badly. (And God doesn't care either way, she said. The person beside you cares, but he's not God, and who cares what he thinks anyway?) Which made me smile in spite of myself.

After the sermon we passed around little white candles, lighting them from each other's, and spoke aloud the names of loved people who had died.

"Julia," I said, so quietly that not even the girl right next to me could have heard it. So quietly that I felt ashamed and pathetic. "Julia," I said again, loud. Loud like when I was absolutely sure of the right answer in class. Loud enough to startle me. But I felt better.

I didn't join in with saying the creeds at the end, even though the girl next to me held out her binder so I could see them. Quakers don't, because it's too easy and too dangerous to turn God into a series of logical propositions. But all around me, the words echoed, "We look for the resurrection of the dead, and the life of the world beyond."

At the memorial I'd heard it without hearing it. It was unbearable, then, to have to set in stone what I believed, to have to organize a whole theology around wishing that she weren't gone. This time I heard that word, "look." Not believe, not be certain, not put an answer on it and stop thinking about it. Just look. That seemed like something I could do.

I came out of the church into the bright clear late-morning sun and tucked my stub of melted white candle in my box of treasures for Julia. I felt like she was watching out for me. I felt like everything was going to be all right even through Arizona and New Mexico and the valley of the shadow of death.

I started to take out the small things I'd been collecting for Julia, just to hold them up to the sun between my fingers and examine them closely. The bits of industrial man-made debris were hard to explain: a grimy shoelace, a battered toy from a Happy Meal, maybe tossed from a car window a year ago. But these are the things that charmed me. They seemed to carry unknowable stories inside them. Stories that even they couldn't know.

Secrets.

I liked that, maybe because I couldn't help feeling like I was keeping secrets from myself.

One time, Julia had a fight with Ollie, and I'd told her every single bad joke I knew and finally said, with more desperation than anything else, "What's brown and sticky?" I saw this tiny smile tug on the corners of her lips, and she blew her nose and wiped her eyes and whispered, "A stick?" Probably she'd been more amused by how hard I was trying than by any joke I could think of, but when Ollie called a couple hours later, he was a little puzzled to hear Julia giggling on the other end of the phone line. And, also, when she asked him what was brown and sticky.

I remembered all those quiet moments that melted into each other: rope swings, watching MTV while we were supposed to be doing our geography homework, running around the neighborhood past midnight just to be delighted that we could, the swimming pool, driving around the city three days after Julia got her license. It was good. Really and truly and honestly. It was good because it was simple, uncomplicated; there weren't any uncomfortable questions or awkward silences. We trusted each other. And once, when someone passed by in the hallway at school whispering something about me being a lesbian, she flirted with me shamelessly until the bell rang, in front of Ollie.

She was that kind of friend.

And the truth is, there was more electricity in those moments than there has ever been, before or since, with anyone else.

I should be able to admit that. I should be able to say that out loud. "Julia," I said, toward a field where there was nothing but a few brown milk cows. "I think maybe—"

And I faltered, because I didn't know what to say.

I was thinking about Jon at the funeral, and what he owed to Julia. If I had anything left to give her at all, it would be to not look away. To risk what I'd come all the way here to risk and let things get more complicated, if they had to. To be able to say, if only to myself, what I really had inside me.

But I couldn't put that in a box where I could give it a label and a meaning so that I could see what direction it was pointing me in. I couldn't put a happy ending on it. It was too late for that now and I didn't even know what a happy ending would look like. I just wanted to find some meaning in the strange things running around inside my heart. I wanted to be able to kneel down with my face in the dirt like an archaeologist and brush the dust off these memories and find out what was true underneath them. It seemed like the least I deserved, when everyone else seemed to have found their direction right away, while I was left wandering. I was one of those people who stumbled into things, who followed whims and took side roads, instead of finding some goal to pursue forward with unflagging commitment. I didn't even know what I wanted to be when I grew up, what I wanted to major in when I went to college. And I had always been blithely convinced that if I followed the side roads for long enough I'd trip over something wonderful, that thing you never know you're looking for until you land on it that suddenly makes the universe a much bigger place than it ever had been before.

I wouldn't find anything if I didn't keep going.

I kept remembering Julia and me lying on the floor of her bedroom, road map spread out between us. Her knees bent so that her little red shoes pointed at the ceiling. "This," she said with conviction, "is going to be fantastic."

Once I'd been buzzed by a car on the way to her house, and my bike fell on top of me, and I couldn't manage to get up again. Four cars passed by without stopping, and the one that stopped was hers, and she held my hand all the way to the emergency room.

I held that in my head. I grabbed that moment and held it close to me like an amulet: the warmth of her hand, and the way it made me forget how my ankle screamed out in pain whenever I moved it the wrong way.

I picked up my bike again, breathing hard. Water bottle on the down tube. Helmet clipped under my chin. Right foot hovering just over right pedal as I glanced back and launched myself over the pavement. Trembling and terrified but moving again, moving *forward*, slowly, both hands grabbing the brakes.

And then the wind grabbed me, and blasted the sweat on my forehead into my eyes, and I was carried off in air and motion.

NOW

It was strange to think that Julia could die and I could bicycle halfway across the country and school would be exactly the same as it always had been. Knots of people just outside the classroom doors, determined to get in every possible word before the bell. Air-conditioning that never worked quite as well as you wished it would, or else too well. I was sweaty from riding to school, and shivered in the too-cold air.

Heather slid into the seat next to mine in first-period English and alternately chewed on her pencil and took notes for the next forty-three minutes, except for when Dr. Vesper had reached the romantic poets section of the syllabus, and she passed me a note that said

Byron and Shelley suck. Am I right?

I answered with a question mark. English wasn't my thing.

We did all this stuff last year.
I can't take it again.
That means you have it easy, I wrote.
Soon you will understand the pain.
BWAH HAH HAH.

She drew a smiley face underneath it with sharp eyebrows and a wide grin, and I couldn't help looking over and grinning back at her.

Later, I passed her in the hall on my way to lunch. She was sandwiched between three other girls, the kind of people you really want to hate, but on top of being pretty and popular and smart and athletic, they're actually nice people. And Gwen too, though unlike them she wasn't too busy taking care of orphaned kittens to pay attention to me. Gwen didn't go out of her way like Heather used to, but if she saw an opening for sarcasm and petty cruelties, she didn't let it get away.

And they were all giggling together.

Yeah. Like I predicted. Heather had found her people in all of half a day.

I stood off to the side and gave Heather a little half wave. "Cass," she said. "I'm just catching up with my friends from middle school—you don't mind, right? I'll see you after school, what room is it?"

"Two eighteen. Sure, it's fine."

There wasn't any way to say that it wasn't fine, and it should have been fine. They were her friends too, even if she hadn't seen them in a while. But it seemed like this was the natural order of the universe, the way to which things would gradually revert. Of course Heather would have better things to do than hang out with the drama geeks.

I went over to the tree where everyone was sitting, and unwrapped my sandwich and grapes and carrot sticks. And we talked about the usual first-day-of-school things, which teachers were rumored to be terrible and whose schedules required the most running back and forth. But I wasn't really there. The last time we had been under this tree sharing anything but a stony silence, the last time we'd been under this tree being silly and happy and kind to each other, Julia had been there. The gaping hole of her gone-ness opened up all at once, and I couldn't bear it.

It was like a betrayal, to think that our lives could keep rolling on without her.

I stayed quiet and smiling, willing myself to not let the others catch my mood, as they kept talking about things that suddenly seemed too small and worthless.

Heather was the last of us to show up at 218, half running with her book bag hanging open. "My eighth period is way on the other end of school. In a trailer. Which, by the way, does not have air-conditioning," she explained, and I didn't want to admit to worrying about whether she was going to show up.

Mr. Vaichon glanced up when we filed in. We came in together, all of us, and he didn't look surprised to see us. "I'm sorry to hear about your ninja thing," he said. "I talked to the principal about it, but I didn't manage to change his mind. If there was anything else I could do—"

"Oh, there is," Heather said brightly.

"The thing is," Lissa said, "we want to volunteer to work on *Our Town*."

"That sounds suspiciously like a non sequitur."

We laid out our plan, piece by piece: We really would help out on *Our Town* and do whatever had to be done. But at the same time, we'd be moving our own props and costumes into the school, and working on our lighting and our sets. *Our Town* wasn't until Thanksgiving— that left most of September and October and almost all of November—so we had plenty of time for both.

"How does the performance fit?" he asked.

"Just have them leave the school open late, like when you're doing dress rehearsals. We'll take care of the rest. And they're going to shut us down after the first night anyway, so there's no point worrying about a full run."

"I can't imagine why this doesn't sound like a good idea."

"We don't want to get anyone in trouble," I said. "But—"

"That's exactly what's going to happen. I'm not going to lie and say I had no idea what was going on."

"Then just say that you're striking a blow for the first amendment," Jon said. "What if you were told you couldn't put on Shakespeare because of the bawdy jokes, or Arthur Miller because of the implied social critique? You wouldn't stand for it, would you?"

"No. But you aren't Shakespeare."

"It's not just a play about ninjas!" Amy protested. "It has love and war and death and secrets and betrayals. Seriously. It's just like Shakespeare."

Ollie had been hanging back till now, with his head down, and his hair flopping in front of his face. Now he slid off the desk he'd been sitting on. "If Julia had lived to be thirty, she'd have been writing the musicals that people will pay a couple hundred dollars to go see. The ones people want to see eight or nine times in a row. That's not going to happen now. So the most we can do for her is to stage *Totally Sweet Ninja Death Squad* in a high school auditorium where it'll be seen by our parents and her parents and a few dozen nerds. We have to do at least that. Otherwise—it'll be like this thing she cared so much about never mattered at all."

"And why, again, did she have to write a musical about violent, ruthless killers?" Mr. Vaichon sighed. "You can do what you like. But I regret this already."

THEN

I rode into Missouri, into the Ozark foothills, and for a long time it was slow going, as I had to muscle my bike up one hill after another, getting off and walking when it got too steep. I was down in a valley late one afternoon when the sky started to cloud over. The air was hot and humid, and then it started to rain, so soft and warm that it was hard to tell the difference between the raindrops and the beads of sweat on my neck.

And then—I felt the bike collapse under me, felt my cheek and my leg hit pavement. No warning. One minute

I was up, the next I was on the road with the bike on top of me. I dragged it to the side of the road and saw where the chain had snapped. I wasn't hurt now, or scared, but I needed to think of a plan, fast. I had tools for changing just about everything that could go wrong with my bike, but I did not have an extra chain, and the pin was bent so that I couldn't fix it with my chain tool. If I could get as far as Springfield, I'd be able to find somewhere to eat, and somewhere to rest, and directions to the nearest bike shop.

Measuring the distance with my finger, it looked like eight or ten miles. Eight or ten miles, that wasn't so bad.

I started walking.

There was something hypnotic about it. One foot in front of the other. One foot in front of the other. Just keep going. Set small landmarks—the next mile marker, the next tree by the side of the road—and just try to get that far. Rolling my loaded bike beside me, I was crawling along incredibly slowly; those eight or ten miles could easily take four hours at this rate.

It wouldn't have been so bad, but the rain started to get heavier the more I went along. Soon the drops were falling so fast and heavy that I had to rummage in my panniers for my poncho. I needed to find shelter. There was no way out but through; I kept walking.

The rain soaked my hands and my legs. Then I felt the water seeping in through the seams of my sneakers. Rain was starting to gather on the ground, ankle-deep in the ditches. And then before I knew it, it was ankle-deep even on the flat ground. My feet started to blister in my wet socks.

If I could just keep going—

An hour passed. The rain kept falling, and the water kept rising. It came halfway to my knees now, so deep and heavy that it was like lugging one of those drowning dummies through a swimming pool, painfully slow. I started thinking that I couldn't do this. I needed a way out now. But I still couldn't see any signs of civilization.

Abruptly, a pickup swerved in front of me, missing me by a couple inches and kicking up a violent spray of water, and stopped on the shoulder.

"What the hell?" I yelled out when I caught my breath.

The passenger-side door swung open. "Get in. It's too dangerous to be out here."

The voice sounded young, female, and I wasn't sure if I should trust it but at least it didn't fit the profile of the average serial killer. And by now I didn't care. The water was going to wash me away.

"My bike," I said.

The other door opened and a girl a couple years older than me climbed out, tall, blonde. She was wearing a holey MSU T-shirt.

Without saying anything, she picked up the bike and tried to heave it into the truck bed.

"It's heavy," I said. I snapped the quick-release for

the front wheel and the back wheel and put them in first—then the panniers—then the frame. It wasn't until we managed to shove it in there that I realized I'd have to take my chances on her being a thief or a maniac or whatever; all of my worldly possessions that I cared about were now in her truck. I wasn't about to leave my bike, so I squeezed into the front seat. A humongous gray husky promptly waggled its way from the back and stuck its nose between my legs.

"Hey, Gin! Down, Gin!" she said with a voice that sounded of defeat, of an absolutely incorrigible dog.

"Your dog's name is Gin?" I asked. "Is there a Tonic?"

"Her full name is Virginia Woolf, but that's just my ex-girlfriend being pretentious, and the dog's not all that smart. As you can tell. So Gin, or Ginny, or Stupid-head."

She hauled the dog away from me by the collar and rubbed her on the head, then started up the truck and took off down the highway. It was too warm inside, with the air conditioner whirring ineffectually and spitting out humid, ozone-scented air, and the warm rain had started to fog up the windows. "I was gonna offer you a ride home, but you're not from around here, are you?"

"I live close to Chicago."

"That's what, eight hours?"

"Something like that."

"Well, you'll stay at my place for the night, and figure what to do from there once the weather's past."

I hesitated. "I can stay at a Motel 6 or something. I've got the cash."

"Not in this weather. The rain'll wash my truck off the road. We're going straight home until it clears up."

"Okay," I finally said. "I'm Cass, by the way. Cassandra. Do you always pick up people at the side of the road?"

"Not always, but I'm usually right about it. That's how I got Gin. And I'm Maggie."

I glanced over at her—one hand on the steering wheel, the other scratching behind Gin's ears, head silhouetted against the rain-splattered window. There was something about her that seemed so sophisticated and mature and sure of herself—her old bumpy truck, or her literary dog, or just the tired way she smiled as she brushed the hair back from her face. Or maybe it was just that she'd rescued me from a flash flood.

She fumbled absentmindedly among a stack of CDs and put one into the CD player, and guitar music started playing, a twangy whisper almost drowned out by the road noise and the splatters of raindrops.

"So, feel free not to answer, but what's the deal? You look kind of young to be stranded this far from home. And in weather like this."

"I'm almost seventeen. And I wasn't stranded."

"You're still young enough to be sticking an *almost* in front of your age. Do your parents know where you are?"

"Roughly," I said. It had been about fifty miles since I'd last called Mom.

"You're lucky if this is as bad as things get."

"I know."

She glanced over at me, just for the half second she could afford when there was rain splattering so thick on the windows I could hardly see out, even with the wipers swishing back and forth. "Please don't tell me you've got parents who don't give a damn what happens to you."

"It's not like that," I said. "They're okay with it. I'm calling home every day. Well, almost."

I had never intended to truly explain myself, because there just wasn't any way to make myself seem reasonable. (And I kind of liked it that way; when I was five hundred miles away from my parents, why in the world should I have to justify my reasonableness to anyone?)

So I waited, and I waited, and I listened to Merle Haggard, and scritched at Gin.

"There was this girl," I said. "I mean—" All of a sudden I felt flustered, and added, "We were just friends."

"No such thing."

"We were."

"Look. Despite what you may have heard, people have sex all the time with people they don't love, or particularly care about, or sometimes can't even stand. So why in the world do people say that it's *just* friends, like it doesn't matter as much, if you're not having sex? Real friendship is true and forever and with all your heart. It's not Relationship Lite."

I nodded slowly. Something inside me went, Oh; it

seemed like she'd just put into words something I'd been stumbling and stumbling over for I don't know how long.

"And you've gone through all of Illinois and most of Missouri on account of this girl who's just a friend. That means something."

"I should have told Oliver that." I wondered if he'd have understood. "But people will talk all day about the virtues of friendship until they get into a relationship themselves."

"Touché." Maggie smiled ruefully.

We pulled up beside a two-story apartment building with dingy vinyl siding. Me, her, and Virginia Woolf went up a flight of stairs to a big studio apartment fitted out with a bed and futon; the walls were covered with postcards, black-and-white photographs, bumper stickers extolling the virtues of organic food, and a few large sketches and watercolors, which put together seemed to cover almost every square inch of the walls of the living/dining/bedroom.

"It's a tight fit," Maggie said, "but the futon's fine to sleep on."

"I'll sleep anywhere. Beats the side of the road, anyway."

She looked at me again with puzzlement that changed almost into admiration. "So, which is it, courage or insanity?"

I shrugged. "I wasn't brave at first. I just didn't care about anything enough to be frightened. And then I started caring, but I kept going anyway because that's the best thing I can think to do. I'm different in real life."

"Since when is this not real life?"

She flicked on the TV, while I went downstairs for my bike. I slid the wheels back on, spent a moment thinking about whether to drag it up the metal stairs along the outside of the building, then locked it underneath them instead, out of the rain. I piled my panniers into my arms and started up the stairs.

Maggie watched dispassionately as I dropped my stuff on the end of the futon, letting it overflow to the floor; I tried to arrange it in some kind of order, but settled for tossing my rolled-up sleeping bag at one end as a pillow.

"Mind if I use your shower?" I was still greasy and smelly and wet and totally unfit for socializing, and it had been bothering me more and more since she'd picked me up.

She nodded absently—so I showered and changed and came back feeling a lot more human, and flopped down next to her on the futon.

"Looks like the worst of it's past, anyway."

Big drops of water were still splattering against the roof and windows, against a sky the color of charcoal.

I nodded. "I just need to get to a bike shop and get a new chain, and then I can be on my way again. But I wouldn't say no to a night out of the rain. If you're sure that's okay."

"Like I'm going to kick you out in this weather just because you're not in mortal danger."

"I go out in the rain all the time." Which wasn't strictly true. I usually tried to catch a ride to school when it rained, and out here I tried to duck into a library or a Walmart or at least into my tent. But I knew what Real Cyclists thought about people who didn't like riding in the rain, and if you were going to be stopped by snow or sleet or dark of night, you at least shouldn't admit it when you were with a much more sophisticated almost-stranger.

"And we have already established that you're not too great at risk-assessment."

"Whatever," I muttered, but I didn't really mind. I liked how it made me feel brave and foolish. "Bikes are safer than cars most ways you look at the statistics."

"Most ways I look at the statistics, the best thing you can do on a day like this is watch TV and drink beer."

"There are statistics on that?"

"Of course. It's empirically provable."

She went over to the fridge, and I watched her with silent interest: an inch of dark roots in her dusty-light hair, a square face set in an expression that could read as annoyance or determination, jeans slung low on her hips.

She returned with two dark bottles, but I waved off the one she held out to me.

"I don't really . . ." I tried to smile. I felt embarrassed and childish all at once, felt that I was in the presence of someone so much cooler and more mature than I would ever be. "Seriously, when I'm at home, I'm the most straitlaced kid you could hope to meet."

And it wasn't that I had never shared when we were over at Ollie's place and someone brought out some grape schnapps, just to taste how awful it was, not because we wanted to get drunk. We had all sampled from Ollie's parents' wine cellar, for a taste of what it was like to be an adult, what it was like to be allowed to do things. Back then it seemed like it was all of a piece with Lissa deciding that she was going to throw a dinner party. Pretending that adulthood was something adorable and hilarious that you could try on for a few hours at a time, not an uncertainty looming closer on the horizon. But this was different, because it was the real thing and not some nervous laugh pointing vaguely at the real thing. I was all on edge. I didn't mistrust her, exactly, but I had started to mistrust myself. However unwise it might have been to set off from home in the first place, going home with a complete stranger was probably the most unwise thing I'd done so far. And I really, really wanted her to like me, because the three or four years she had on me seemed like forever, a future I could hardly conceive of for myself, and everything about her was so much cooler than I could aspire to. So there was the more reasonable part of my brain, the part that could quote safety statistics, telling me stop it. Be suspicious. Be square.

"Suit yourself."

I got some water from the tap and sat down again,

squirming on the futon trying to find a comfortable position. "She's dead now," I said.

Maggie blinked at me.

"My friend, the girl I was talking about before."

"And that's why a straitlaced girl like you is out playing Lance Armstrong five hundred miles from home."

"Sort of," I said. "It wouldn't have been so bad if I had friends. I thought I did. But it turns out I was just borrowing them from her."

"And when you're gone they'll all realize that they should have been nicer to you?"

"No!" I said quickly. "It's not like that. I need to find a way to memorialize her, and I have to do it by myself."

My fingers traced patterns in the futon's wood grain. I was leaning so far over the side that the frame bit into my waist and my arms and my hips. Like I was trying to get away, almost, but I didn't want to get away.

"A way to memorialize her," Maggie repeated. "For that, you had to come all the way out to . . . where are you going anyway?"

"I'm going to California. Santa Monica."

She laughed, a dry chuckle. I looked up. Her eyebrow arched skeptically, but she smiled with deep gentleness. "It's been a while since I checked, but I seem to remember some mountains and some desert in the way."

"I'll figure out how to deal with those when I get there." I no longer sat down with maps and a calculator almost every night to try to persuade myself one way or the other—would I get there, would I succeed, would I fail, should I turn back. There wasn't really a question of turning back now.

And still, I got out my maps, and I got out my calculator. Maggie pointed out just where we were, and I counted 1,692 miles from here to there. Fifty-eight days, so twenty-nine miles a day. I was making good time, except that I should be making better time to make up for how the desert would slow me down. But I would fix my bike, and I would get back on the road, and it would be all right.

The sky lightened slowly, and darkened slowly. Maggie finished most of her beer and poured the rest into the slow cooker for flavor. We ate. We watched ancient sitcoms and talked cautiously over the commercials.

"I'm not in school anymore," she said, when I asked. "I did that for two years, and then my folks decided that if I was going to get all kinds of weird ideas in my head, that was okay, but I could do it on my own dime. So, here I am fussing over whether you parents know where you are, even though mine sure don't." And she laughed it off the same way Jon laughed it off when his parents were on his case, the way you have to pretend it's something you're strong enough to laugh off. "Anyway, when I looked at my own dimes I had about three of them. So for the past year I've been working here and there and figuring out what to do next. Mostly at the Market. Oh, we should go there tomorrow, definitely.

They make these peach scones—and vegan ginger cookies—and you can stock up on supplies, if you need some energy bars, or some fair trade socks."

"Okay," I said. I don't know why I said that. I was supposed to go to the bike shop and put a chain on my bike and get on my way.

I was intrigued by her.

I discovered myself watching her, watching her ragged chewed fingernails and the electric blue polish that was peeling off her toenails, watching her fingers knot in her hair, watching her stretch out leisurely over her half of the futon.

I was intrigued most of all by how I watched her. I didn't think that I had ever watched somebody like that before. Julia, well—Julia was my friend. I was careful to omit the *just* when I thought it this time. But I could hardly remember discovering her, could hardly remember her being new to me. I'd never needed to scrutinize her like I was scrutinizing Maggie, trying to figure out the vast sea of what I didn't know from what was right in front of me. This was new—and I didn't want to stop just yet.

On the second day of se-
nior year, I was still trying to figure out where I stood with
Heather. I couldn't really blame her if she wanted to eat
lunch with other people, after spending the entire summer
with us, but I couldn't imagine her wanting to spend more
than a day with her friends from middle school. And just
because she was still friends with them didn't mean things
were going to be like they were before—right?

But after third period I saw Heather a few steps
in front of me, going to lunch again with Gwen and
Groupies. I could hear snatches of talking, and it was

all the same stuff as always. Whose personal life was a complete train wreck, and who had the misfortune of getting asked out by a guy whose only interest seemed to be collecting Magic cards, and how lame everything and everyone was.

I shouldered past them, thinking that Heather would just keep going, but in a minute she'd caught up with me.

"I'm allowed to be friends with them," she said.

"I didn't say you weren't."

"You were glaring. Incandescently."

I didn't want to be this person who glared. I didn't want to create drama out of who she was friends with. But did she really think that she was going to be exempt from their judgment just because she used to be friends with them? Did she think they would go easy on her? "Gwen is the kind of girl who's just waiting for a moment of weakness. The other two, I don't know. I guess I'm beneath their notice. But she's not going to be okay with you."

We escaped the crush of bodies in the hallway and stood outside under the eaves. I could see the oak tree from where we were, and Jon sitting under it, but I didn't start in his direction. "I know that," Heather said. "But at least around them I don't have to be on my toes pretending to be a saint, and I don't have to watch what I say every minute in case I accidentally let slip something that's a little mean."

The way she looked at me told me that, yes, that was a little mean, and no, it wasn't an accident.

"Are you sure about that?" I asked.

"Don't," she said. And then, quietly, "Don't tell me."

I shrugged. "I don't have anything to say to you that you don't know already. Except you've got better friends than that, if you want them."

"I don't know why it has to be so hard," Heather whimpered, almost defeated. "I went through middle school and I said I wasn't going through that again. And I went through three years of Catholic school and I said I wasn't going through that again. But I'm still hearing this voice in my head telling me that I could have it easy and I could be popular and—I don't know how I'm supposed to not want that."

"I'd probably want that too," I admitted.

"So I guess I should tell them I'm a thespian, and watch them be very confused?" She tried to smile. "Come on, I have an announcement." And we walked over to the tree.

"Hey, everybody, listen up," Heather said. "Today after school, we will be having a demonstration of costumes, props, special effects, and weaponry. Be there. Or else."

"Since when?" I asked.

"Since I said so. Everything's ready, right?"

"Right, but—"

"Then it is officially time to show off your artillery

skills. So we'll meet over at the theater after school."

I wanted to say no. Just today, just for this moment when I wanted life to stop for a while and give me time to catch up. I was still a little mad, and Heather was pretending nothing was wrong even though it wasn't true.

"It's been a long day. And it's only lunch."

"Yeah, but you don't have any homework yet, right? It'll be fun, promise!"

I think I said yes because I wasn't expecting that. Heather knew when to leave me alone in my moods—even if you could tell she was trying to be subtle about it—but other times she was pushy when she had a good reason to be pushy.

And it was true that I didn't have any homework yet.

She got there before I did; how long, I don't know, but by the time I got there she was leaning against the side of the building and staring off into the distance watching for me, dressed in her pretty brocade kimono, which was hiked up on her shins so that the edges wouldn't trail in the grass.

"What does that thing get, three miles an hour?"

"Twelve, with flat ground and not too much wind in my face."

"You couldn't put, like, an engine on it or something?"

"For that money I'd rather get a new Bianchi. I could get up to eighteen or twenty on it."

"Well, you could paint flames on the sides, at least. C'mon, everybody's waiting for you."

While I loaded up the miniature catapults with artillery and set up my booby traps, Lissa was passing out costumes, holding them up to measure against the other actors—yards and yards of black silk, or not silk but the shiny artificial stuff that costs three bucks a yard, and there were individual details on each costume, a thin trim of yellow or pink or scarlet, appliqué or embroidery on the sleeves. And colored sashes, of course, to tell all the characters apart from far back in the audience. Rainbow for Jon, and orange for Amy, and for Lissa a sedate sage green. Heather's was bright pink. Amy cooed in appreciation and tied the orange sash around her waist.

Oliver wasn't cooing. Fine, I didn't really expect him to coo. He just watched, resting his head in his hands, an inscrutable expression on his face. I kept wondering if this could really be real—if two weeks from now Jon and Heather and Ollie would be onstage, and the strange small orchestra we'd gathered would be playing, and my booby traps would detonate when they were supposed to. I'd seen school plays come together, of course. I'd seen that moment when a bunch of people of varying levels of talent suddenly clicked and created the illusion of something magical. But always with adults to watch over it; this felt very much like walking right up to the edge of the cliff.

Except that Oliver was the one who was leading us to the brink. Did he think about these things too? Or was he certain that he could make everything work okay, somehow?

All the lights were on, furiously bright and ugly, and they seemed to double the size of every place where someone's brush had slipped or the jigsaw had cut a too-jagged line. But I wasn't going to apologize for that.

Amy poked at the castle ramparts, weaving in and out of the little hiding spots. "This is just like in the script! And this is where Loud Ninja and Buddhist Ninja hide when they're trying to eavesdrop on Hiromasa to figure out if he's really on their side or not. Oh—and the ninja fort in the trees!"

And I set off the remote-controlled gadgets that could spring open and spring shut, or launch imagined arrows into the air.

Jon experimented with creeping stealthily around the booby traps. Lissa followed with her shoes off, and squeaked when she brushed up against the little lever in the wall that made an arrow fly just over her head. But Oliver's face stayed glassy and frozen.

Well, that was okay. I put a carefully constructed smile on. "The niftiest things, if you ask me, are these little hand catapults. You can carry them around like this, and you can aim them at things, and fire them—"

Nothing happened when I flicked the switch.

Nothing.

"Okay, technical difficulties, no problem, it'll be fixed soon. Um, Heather?" I asked. "Pass me the other one?"

I took it from her and loaded it with Ping-Pong balls. This time it worked, this time little balls flew in every direction across the room.

But it didn't matter. The spell was broken, and I didn't have it in me to keep up the front of cheerfulness when Oliver was staring into the distance with those hollow eyes.

And as the rest of them clapped politely, Oliver turned and started up the stairs.

"Hey," I called out, and when he didn't even look back I followed him. "What is it?"

"It's nothing," he said. "It's fine. You're right. You'll get it fixed."

"I promise, I will."

"Anyway—everything looks different when you've got the distance from the audience to the stage. No one is going to notice."

"It's fine."

But I had seen things through his eyes; everything started to look desperately cheap and slapdash and not good enough. I knew he didn't mean it. And no, I wasn't going to let it go at that—not after all the work I'd gone through, the sandpaper scratches and knife cuts on my hands. No, I wasn't going to let myself stew in not-good-enough.

"I'm not going to let you down on this. I know what this means to you and I'm not going to screw up. So can you stop pretending that you don't care? Can you just talk to me honestly for a second?"

"Who said I wasn't being honest?" Ollie asked. He titled his head down, hiding behind his hair.

I snorted. "You do the whole sensitive-guy-who-talks-about-his-feelings thing well enough, when it suits you. It's not fair to hide behind gloomy monosyllables now."

His mouth quirked. "Since when do I do the sensitive guy thing?"

"Since Julia was all moony over you. She did tell me some things, you know. Otherwise I wouldn't have cheered for you guys."

Oliver heaved open the big steel door and sat down on the steps by the theater's back door. I sat down beside him, my fingers resting on the hot sun-baked bricks.

"You cheered for us? Really?"

"That is so completely, utterly, and totally beside the point that I don't know where to start. But, yeah. One, I desperately wanted to find out what all this romance stuff was like without the hassle of personally getting involved with someone, so having you as Julia's boyfriend gave me something to learn from besides really bad television. And, two, you are not an asshole or an idiot, you didn't make fun of her interests, you didn't cheat on her, and you didn't indulge in locker-room jock-boy bragging."

"You're really setting the bar high there."

"Also, I am obviously a huge expert on relation-ships."

Yes. Finally got a smile out of him, even if it was just a little one.

"Like that decrepit old lady who gives sex advice on late-night TV."

"Hey," I said. Mock-offended. "Unlike me, she actually knows what she is talking about."

Oliver got quiet then. He opened his mouth as if to say something, and closed it again.

I cautiously reached over and put my hand on his shoulder. He sighed, his eyes pointedly turned away from me.

"Cass," he said. "I'm terrified."

"Because of the play?"

He nodded.

"Look, everybody is a nervous wreck when they're doing a play. Especially when they're trying to produce, direct, and act. It makes you insane. Look at Mel Gibson."

"Except that I'm completely unqualified to do any of those things, except maybe the acting."

"But you survived *Oklahoma!* when the wind came sweeping over the plains and knocked over a set. And last summer at drama camp, didn't you survive when the flaky director chick decided it would be awesome to have real cats in *Cats* even though one of the leads was so allergic he nearly had to go to the hospital?"

"This time it's my responsibility, though. Whatever goes wrong is my fault."

"Nobody said it had to be perfect."

I said it, and I realized that I was wrong. "It's Julia."

"She wrote and arranged a musical in four months.

While staying on the honor roll and rehearsing a play and getting in fights with me because she'd rather work on her super-secret project than go out on the weekend. Do you realize how amazing that is? I have no idea how to live up to that."

The shadows had crept an inch across my hand while we were talking. I wondered if Heather and the rest of them had gone home yet, or if they were still camped out in the basement trying to pretend everything was okay.

I didn't want to give him some stupid platitude about how it only mattered that we were all doing our best.

"Do you realize that she rhymed 'love' and 'dove' in one of those songs?"

"'Maybe I Won't Kill You,' verse three. I *have* been rehearsing this thing for the last few months."

"It's just, she asked me to shoot her if she ever wrote such a banal and overdone rhyme."

"Obviously she wouldn't have asked *you*, if she really meant it."

I had to smirk, just a little, at that.

"The point is, she might have had this idea in her head of a great musical epic. But even if she was scary-smart, and even if what she wrote is a lot more entertaining than half of what's on Broadway, it's not this perfect little thing with all the edges polished. It still has all the fuzzy bits and rough bits and weird bits in it."

"I don't care about that."

"Me neither. Because, the thing is, she did care about

being great. But she was happy just to write something with love and revenge and violence and cool costumes and exciting twists, and parts for you and Jon and Lissa and Amy and even a little place for me chiseled out in a corner. And when you listen, you know that she gave us . . . herself."

For the first time Ollie looked into my eyes. He nodded slowly, his whole face tensed.

"I can hear her in all of it. In the arpeggios and the chord changes and the lyrics and the instrumentation. It's *her*. That's why it's so hard."

"But that's why it doesn't have to be perfect. It just has to be from you . . . and from me, and from all of us. Then we won't betray her even if someone suddenly blanks on every single one of their lines, or the cellist accidentally knocks out the guy beside him."

He ruffled my hair. He was even smiling, though I could see in his eyes that he was trying really hard to hold it together. "Thanks for the pep talk."

"At least our costumes will be awesome."

"Lissa's a genius. And Heather's not bad either, even though she's only doing some of the hemming and lining and edging."

"Huh," I said. Of course, that was true. I'd known that already, but somehow I hadn't connected it in my mind with Heather down in the basement with me all the time, squinting at her stitching in the bad light.

It shouldn't have taken her so long. She didn't have

to be down there. It didn't seem so strange, now that we were friends, now that we sometimes had to remind each other to pry ourselves away from talking and get back to work. But she had haunted the basement even when I could hardly look at her, when I would cross the room to get a tool that she could've handed to me. It wasn't so easy to think now that it was as simple as needing any place to get work done.

"Thank you," Ollie said. "For trying so hard to get along with Heather."

"Oh."

"What, oh?"

It hadn't been that long. August when I came back, September now—not much more than a month. Hardly more than a month, and I couldn't even tell Oliver how much had changed.

"I'm not really trying so hard," I said with a laugh. "We talked things over, and—we're good now, I guess."

"How did that happen?" Oliver asked, eyes wide.

I shook my head. "Doesn't matter." I had no wish right now to expose all of Heather's secrets, which she'd spent carefully like precious currency to win my trust or make me believe she'd suffered enough. "People change. Apparently people change more than I thought."

"You're smiling."

"Yeah, I guess I am." Suddenly I felt blushy and embarrassed and I didn't want to say anything more about it. "What, I'm not allowed to smile?"

"Okay, okay." Ollie held his hands up in surrender. "I am officially not pressing the issue anymore, starting now."

I wanted to say something to him. I almost did. But it was still too complicated, still the wrong time. Maybe after the play was done, I would let myself think about this again, and say something, to someone.

Not now.

But at home, curled up on my bed with a bowl of apple slices, I took the beat-up script for *Totally Sweet Ninja Death Squad* out of my backpack. And I pushed myself through all the parts that used to make my stomach clench up because I couldn't take being reminded that much of Julia, the ninjas who could divide by zero and every other silly joke that almost no one but us would have understood.

It was hers. And it was for me too. And it hurt, but I found that I could bear it after all. I found that I didn't want to hide from those memories.

When I was done, and I'd checked to make sure that absolutely no one was at home, I opened up to the sheet music and started singing.

THEN

I woke up on Maggie's futon and, for the first time in weeks, spent the morning doing absolutely nothing. It was wonderful to be so lazy, just this once—I was not so cold or hot or restless or tired or melancholy or lonely that I had to push myself forward to whatever was waiting for me next. It was already past eleven by the time I managed to get showered and dressed, and even then Maggie had to make a pointed comment or two about when her shift started.

She cruised slowly down the main street, pointing out the Market and the creepy toy store and Pedal Power, the local bike shop, where she dropped me off. It was a small enough town that it only took three minutes to see what there was to see, but it felt bigger and more interesting than that. Because of the university close by, Maggie said—it was swarming with grad students and college burnouts.

"So, um—" I hauled my bike out of the truck bed, and it clattered on the ground. "I guess I'll drop by the Market after I'm done here, and then when you get off work I'll go get my stuff from your place."

She shook her head. "May as well stay the night. It'll practically be dark by then."

"It's too much of an imposition."

"Then you can walk the dog. But this is the last outpost of human civilization for the next fifty miles. No reason to rush through it."

I did miss civilization. And human beings. I didn't want to admit it, but I did.

"Okay," I said finally. "If you say so. Thanks."

I spent an hour in the back room of Pedal Power. It was a comfortable place, like the shop I'd once visited every weekend to see the blue-green Bianchi in just my size. They sold practical city bikes with racks and fenders, not just slim feather-light racing bikes and mountain bikes that were unlikely to ever see a mountain, and they had cycling advocacy pamphlets on display racks and a Help Wanted sign in the window. The owner let me in back to put on my new chain, and I spent the rest of my time rubbing off the mud caked onto the frame and dripping oil into the moving parts. It didn't matter too much that my bike would only get muddy again in a couple days; I felt bright inside, with the urge to do a million things at once. In the absence of a million things that needed doing, I could at least take proper care of my bike.

Later I traced my way back to the Market. It was a big store bordering a lawn, with a tin awning sheltering a patio with metal tables and chairs. Old hounds were lounging under trees, their tongues hanging out; a shaggy-haired boy was strumming a guitar badly. Which reminded me of Kris, and made me feel complicated. Shouldn't I care more about that? Shouldn't I feel something more than a twinge of uncertainty?

I ducked into the store and wandered among the aisles picking out the things I'd forgotten or run out of, sunscreen, just-add-hot-water meals, gas for the little camp stove, pomegranate-flavored ChapStick, an extra pair of wool socks hand-knit somewhere in the Andes; then Maggie waved me over and led me to a little table in the café. She brought me a slice of peach cobbler and vanilla ice cream and collapsed into the chair beside me.

"Nice place, right?"

I nodded. "It's been nearly a month since I've stayed anywhere more than long enough to do laundry. I started daydreaming about dry socks and food that isn't rehydrated."

Which was only the uncomplicated part of the truth.

"Aren't you sick of it by now?"

I shrugged. "It doesn't matter if I'm sick of it or not. I'm here because I have a job to do and I'm too stubborn to give up on it. And also," I admitted, "it beats the alternative."

"Really? July temperatures and complete strangers versus central air-conditioning and friends and family?"

"I'll take complete strangers right now." I poked with my fork at the caramelized remnants of peach cobbler. "The problem when you know people is that they know you, or they think they know you, and suddenly you can't dye your hair or say a curse word without them all getting together to work their Freudian mojo and figure out what's wrong with you and how to fix it." Pause. "And whether you can be expected to put the moves on your best friend."

Maggie smiled a pained smile at me. "God, I'm glad I'm not in high school anymore."

"Don't be the eightieth person to tell me it's going to get better. I'm getting tired of that line."

"Seriously. You can be a Marxist stamp collector if you want to be a Marxist stamp collector and anyone who would give you a hard time for that is out getting tattooed and protesting homework or the sweatshop that makes the student clothing or the war."

I beamed at that. "You know, I had the best war protest signs ever, when I was twelve. They were pink and blue and covered with glitter. Like a really outraged

Hello Kitty. My parents' hippie friends thought I was adorable." My parents too, though they complained for weeks that they were still vacuuming up glitter.

Maggie's eyes widened for a second, and she let out a small, embarrassed laugh.

"What?"

"You were *twelve* when the war started. That's so young. I don't think I know anyone who went to a protest with their parents' hippie friends."

"So? What difference does that make? I mean, I know I'm not sophisticated enough to name my dog Virginia Woolf—"

"Hey, me neither," Maggie said with a shrug. "My ex was the lit major. It doesn't make a difference, I guess. As long as your folks know where you are and aren't hunting all up and down the Midwest for you."

I said they weren't. I checked my voicemail just to make sure. The automatic voice said no new messages, and I didn't want to admit the twinge I felt, of being just a little bit lonely and unsure and wanting to hear a familiar voice. It was too childish.

"You spend a long time wishing that your parents would just get out of your life and leave you alone," Maggie said. "But then they do, and you wish they'd get in your face again. Maybe just once, so you can remember how rotten it felt."

"Really?" I asked, and it occurred to me that she wasn't just talking about me.

She shrugged, like maybe she didn't want to admit it either, and let the subject drop until that night. I'd offered to walk Ginny before, but after I got the leash out of the closet the dog was bouncing around so much I couldn't manage to clip it on.

Maggie grabbed her by the collar to hold her still. "I'd better go with you. She doesn't get tired until she's been out for two miles, and that's far enough to get lost."

"You don't have to."

But she went outside with me anyway. The air was still hot, the sky just starting to turn a deeper shade of blue. The dog picked her own direction, following the two-lane highway out of town, snuffling at the fast-food wrappers tossed from passing cars.

"Idiot drivers," Maggie muttered. "You sure you want to bike on this road?"

"Mostly it's not so bad if you ride like you know you're allowed to be there. And I can react pretty quickly if I'm paying attention. Stupid maybe, but it's not actively murderous."

"Well," she said dubiously. "Would you send me an e-mail every now and then just so I know you're not dead?"

"I'm not going to die." I said it before I had time to realize how wrong it was, the glib assumption that we were all immortal until proven otherwise. How Julia was probably certain that she wasn't going to die either. "Okay, though. I will."

I should've sent an e-mail to everybody by now. An e-mail, at least, even if I wasn't going to call them. I'd said I would, but somehow whenever I stopped at a library and managed to get time on a computer, I froze up and spent the half hour gathering my courage. And then I posted my GPS coordinates in my journal online, and that was it.

"And be careful, would you?"

"I know."

"You're lucky to have parents who don't mind you doing your own thing for a while. Mostly, the kids I knew who used to do crazy stuff were the ones whose parents were drunk or had their own problems or just didn't give a damn. And I don't know if there's something you haven't told me, but that's not you, right?"

"No. They just trust me to figure things out for myself right now."

"Yeah. I heard you talking on the phone before, with your mom." She stuffed her hands in her pockets and sighed. "When I was your age—and that's a terrible way to start off saying anything, but when I was your age I wouldn't have been okay without my family that long. We were really close, all of us. I didn't even fight with my dad about the usual stupid stuff like curfews and clothing. Didn't want to go out of town for college."

Maggie pointed vaguely northward. "I grew up over there, about twenty minutes away in a car. Haven't been back in over a year now. Haven't talked with my dad in months. And I hear you on the phone, just saying you're fine, you're in Missouri still, you got socks and a new chain for your bike. I miss being able to say that."

I wasn't going to ask about what happened. I was capable of putting the pieces together. Or they were different pieces, harder ones to talk about, and I didn't see how it made sense to poke at it just to watch the carnage.

I remembered the fallout after Jon had come out of the closet, when he'd gone to stay with Julia's family for a few days until things started to blow over. I went to her place the next afternoon and he said very firmly, "I've talked about what happened six times. Which is exactly six times too many."

"Okay," I'd said. "What should I do?"

"Help me conquer South America?"

So we gathered around the computer and gave him advice about how many tanks to build, and how many airplanes, and by the time he'd conquered our continental neighbors, he had stopped with the compulsive fidgeting and agreed to eat an actual meal.

I ended up recounting the whole saga, or as much of it as I knew, to my parents. I was fourteen then but still feeling out where they stood on some things, having gotten a long lecture a few months before for asking if we were Communists.

And what happened is that we invited Jon over for dinner, and talked mostly about computer games and hardly at all about how he didn't want to go back home.

It was true, I was awfully lucky.

"The last couple of months," Maggie said, "have been the first time in my entire life I haven't been fighting with someone about when I could shower, or what was a reasonable time to turn the TV off, or who was going to wash the dishes. And it sucks. You would not think that a studio apartment could feel that big and empty, especially when you're sharing it with a dog the size of a pony, but it does."

"I know," I said. "A person leaves, and—their goneness is so huge. You keep tripping into it."

"So, it's been good having you here. There's something reassuring about just having someone else in the same room."

We'd wound over the roads for a while by now, and made our way back to her apartment. She fumbled in her pocket for her keys, but didn't unlock the door.

"I'm not asking you to stay for a while or anything. You've got places to go, obviously. It's just. If you wanted to."

I shook my head, and then I looked up at her and I realized this wasn't really about whether I felt like taking another day or two doing as little as possible. And I felt very dense, all of a sudden, to have spent these past two days watching her like I'd been watching her, and not seeing that until now.

"Forget that I said anything." She smiled ruefully.

"You're just a kid. You don't need to be hearing at great length about my personal issues."

"I am not," I said—the stupidest thing I could have said. Of course.

But it made her smile.

And she brushed her lips up against mine.

I stood there blinking at her, motionless, trying not to say anything I shouldn't say.

"I probably shouldn't have done that," she said.

"No," I said. "You probably should've." I felt quieter, and more certain, than the time before in the hotel with Kris. But I was grinning, too much, on the outside.

"There's no way I can take responsibility for some poor confused kid."

"No one's asking you to take responsibility for me." I stretched out and touched my palm to her chin, and I could feel my fingers tremble when I kissed her with all the enthusiasm of someone who'd only just discovered kissing. She kissed me back like she meant it, her breath hot and near.

"I came into this trip clear-eyed with the idea that I would not back down from whatever terrible thing happened to befall me. And I'm still not backing down. Not that this is any kind of terrible thing."

"But you are leaving."

"Not until tomorrow."

"Do you really think you can make it all that way by yourself?"

I didn't have any kind of an answer for that question.

Yes, yes, I believe it, I know it. And I know I'm wrong. But I believe it anyway.

How could I say that?

"It doesn't matter whether I can," I said finally. "It doesn't matter whether I think I can. I'm going. That's all."

I said that. But the truth was that I had never felt so doubtful about whether I really could, not even in my bleakest moments.

She hesitated as she unlocked the door, stepped inside, turned the air conditioner on. "Well, you don't have to leave at the crack of dawn. Really, I'll make waffles."

I couldn't help but smile, because she charmed me and because I didn't want her to see my doubt, my fear. I had to remind myself that I really couldn't stay. I really couldn't. I had to say it out loud to convince myself.

"So stay a day," she said. "Stay two days. This isn't like high school where you kiss someone and you start thinking all the way forward to forever, complete with two dogs in the yard."

I told myself that I would run the calculations. I told myself that I would make sure I stayed on track.

I felt like I could tell her the truth. "I have absolutely no idea what I'm doing."

"That's two of us."

Maggie curled her arm around me, and I nestled in closer to her, but truthfully I was comfortable there because she did know what she was doing, or at least she knew how to make it seem that way. She stretched out like a lazy, contented cat—and there was just a little protectiveness in her hand on my shoulder. And she made me think that she had kissed lots of people before, and it wasn't the kind of huge thing that should be making my stomach turn over, even if my stomach didn't understand that yet.

This is the kind of thing that makes people wink knowingly and say, "Yeah, I'm sure," but this is all that happened: We stayed up and watched David Letterman and *South Park,* and we kissed during all the commercial breaks, and when I was tired and shivery and stupid with everything that had happened, Maggie retreated from the futon to the bed and turned out the lights.

NOW

After school the next day, I went back to the hand-catapult that had stuck the day before. By poking and prodding it, eventually I found the place where two pieces were rubbing against each other. I sanded the pieces smooth again, loosened and tightened, until the whole mechanism flowed smooth as water.

I was so absorbed in the work that I didn't realize Heather had come down into the basement until I looked up.

"Oliver was such a jerk yesterday. You shouldn't let him get to you."

I hadn't even been thinking about him. I'd been thinking about her. What I should say to her, if I should say anything to her, even though I kept telling myself it wasn't the right time. And getting nervous because in a couple of weeks we'd be done with the play, and I wouldn't have that excuse.

"It's no big deal," I said. "We worked things out."

"And now we have a working catapult. Which is to say, now that function is dealt with, we can think about form . . ."

"You saw it too, didn't you?" I asked, getting out a dustpan to sweep up the bits of sawdust and wood shavings on the floor.

"Saw what?"

"We can't have all the sets looking like we saved up our lunch money to build them. Not if we can improve on that, in the time we have left."

Heather pressed her fingers to her lips. "Mind if I try something?"

"I'll trust your sense of style over mine. You're all done with your sewing?"

"Done, and thank God. I never want to see any ribbon or any lace, ever again. My fingers just can't face another needle." She held them up, but the light wasn't very good—I had to get a lot closer to her before I saw all the little pricks on her fingertips.

And I realized how close I was to her, and how my

hands were nearly touching hers. I took a step back. "Okay, what's the plan?"

"Not so much a plan," Heather admitted. "More of an experiment. Clear out a space on the floor over there."

While I worked on picking up bits of props, she waded through stacks of old crates and re-emerged carrying a roll of dingy canvas. "I've seen this around before. I don't know if it's worth using, but—"

"Can we?"

"I ran into one of the guys who's in charge here. He said no one had any idea why it was there or what it was originally bought for, and we could do whatever we wanted with it."

She unrolled it upside down, with the less dusty side showing, but it was frayed at the edges and a little yellow. I wasn't sure about this.

"We want to start in the *middle* so that we don't trap ourselves while waiting for the paint to dry. You'd think that would be obvious, but it's not so much."

Heather pointed at a can by all the other cans of paint. "First, we cover it with black. Like those pretty Japanese lacquer boxes."

"We've already got a black backdrop," I said, just a little dubiously.

"Trust me," Heather replied, like someone with a secret too good to keep. "I mean, I don't know if this is going to work or not, but I can't resist trying it out."

We got to work. We started out right beside each other, taking small slow steps toward the edges as we went along. Once in a while I looked up at her just to see her intense concentration, her tongue just barely sticking out between her lips, and the way she crouched over gracefully—or the reckless way she dragged her paintbrush across big swatches of the canvas. For a second I nearly felt guilty, because I liked her and I wasn't saying anything, and if she knew she would pull down at the pink T-shirt that was creeping up on her midriff, or she wouldn't let herself sprawl carelessly on the floor like she did. So I went back to my painting as soon as I noticed—not before I noticed the silvery cross dangling on her pale neck.

"I'm going to be really nosy now."

"What's left to be nosy about?" She almost laughed.

"Are you still Catholic?"

"Oh, that," she said, looking down at her chest with a sigh. "Well—some days yes and some days no. Today happens to be a yes day."

"Even though—?"

"Yeah. You've heard of cafeteria Catholics?"

I shook my head.

"Ever been to a cafeteria with one of those people who's really annoying because they're vegetarian, and allergic to this, and can't stand to eat that, and eww, the Jell-O has a skin on it, so they end up sitting at the table with three limp lettuce leaves and a slice of tomato? Kind of like that. So I complain and complain about my lettuce and tomato. And there are times I would rather be complaining about my lettuce and tomato than going somewhere else where I can eat what I want. So—that's hard to explain, and I guess it doesn't make much sense. The part that's easy to explain is that as long as I am in that house I am going to Mass on Sunday, *young lady.*"

She shrugged it off, but I couldn't help thinking of all the history I didn't know and couldn't bring myself to ask about.

"When did you stop thinking it was wrong?"

"Being a lesbian?"

I hesitated. "Yeah."

"Not until Gianna," she said, after a long pause. "For a long time I could pretend to think about it abstractly. I just about convinced myself it was about obscure points of theology, not about my own real life and my future and whether I would ever kiss someone on the mouth. Then I saw how sad and scared and hurting Gianna was, and for the first time I got angry with the unfairness of it all. And when I was done with being angry, I was done with being scared too. One of us had to be."

She kept painting for a while. "Your parents are pretty strict, aren't they? About TV and makeup and all that?"

"Well, they didn't want me getting my moral compass from people who are only interested in selling me something. But love is different. If two people care about each other, and take care of each other, they wouldn't ever say a word against that. And there were usually gay people around at our meeting, and they always just treated it like something normal."

"Wait," Heather said, starting to grin. "You're not allowed to set foot in Sephora, but you're allowed to be gay?"

"They're big on hippie Jesus, you know? Turn the other cheek, love your enemies." I stopped short, because I hadn't meant to say "love," didn't want to say anything that could be about her. I backed away from that subject. "Anyway, I'm going to be seventeen next month. If I really want to wear sparkly purple eye shadow, I'm not going to sneak around applying it in the school bathrooms."

She shook her head and went back to my first statement. "There's gotta be a limit to turning the other cheek, or you just get people trying to walk all over you."

"It's not about just sitting around hoping that things will get better. It's that—if you believe in God like my dad does, if you believe that we're only seeing a tiny sideways glance at all the things that are working themselves out for the best in the end, then there's no point in flailing around trying to make things better by killing people. It's like when you're trying to cut your own hair, and it doesn't look right, so you just cut more and more trying to fix it, and it just keeps getting worse. Except, you wind up with dead people."

"But what about you? You don't believe that?"

"I don't know. I believe in God sometimes, but I can't just say for sure that everything's going to be okay. It's too glib. It's like the people who are hurting right now don't count for anything. But I do know that I want to live in the kind of world where people can get past getting even with each other. I want to live in the kind of world where people can manage to love their enemies." And I didn't back off from it that time.

It took the better part of the day to finish getting paint in all the corners we could reach. We didn't quite have enough room on the floor to spread out the entire width of the canvas, so we left the outside edges for later, when the wet paint dried and we could roll it up in the middle. After we finished, we stretched out in the grass outside, sucking down ice and lemonade in the September heat.

"What now?"

"Well, it should be dry in a couple of days. So, come back Friday night. We'll finish up."

Friday. Friday, exactly two weeks before the premiere.

We had two weeks and two days. Twelve school days to finish up all the sets and the lighting for *Totally Sweet Ninja Death Squad*—and keep working on *Our Town* as promised—staying late after school every day, working every weekend on what we could do without sneaking into school.

"We're gonna make it, right?"

"Of course," Heather said. "Of course."

We kept busy until Friday, plastering the school with posters and flyers for the real performance of *Our Town* (with a handwritten note scrawled in: Special sneak preview, September 19!), hauling our props and pieces of the set into the school. No one cared or paid us much attention. We were just the drama nerds, putting on a play nobody really cared about.

Except for the persistent rumor, which we all denied while raising our eyebrows conspiratorially (and then confirmed in whispers after swearing everyone to secrecy), that the special sneak preview was going to be something a little different.

So the community theater was empty that afternoon when me and Heather went down into the basement, her in a white apron that proclaimed IRON CHEF, me in old clothes that could get splattered with paint. I went down in darkness, my hand pressed against the railing and my toes searching out the steps; then Heather flicked the lights on.

The black backdrop hung on thumbtacks across the entire width of the wall. Around it—I had to get up close to see the detail properly; there were curlicues and elegant flowing strokes of gold, and painstakingly etched flowers and feathers, and when I looked closer I saw the tones of scarlets and oranges that stood out against the black.

But it was the image at the center that was so beautiful I nearly had to sit down from surprise. A bright phoenix, rising up from flames, and so alive it seemed like it could pop off the wood.

"So, um. There isn't actually anything left for me to do, is there?"

She just grinned at me. "Is it okay?"

I kept staring. "Okay. Yeah. It's . . . a little more than okay. How did you do this? When?"

"Paint and stencils? When you thought the paint was drying?"

Obviously I was asking the wrong questions. "Why?"

"Because—because—I felt like I wanted to do something good, for you. Because really all I was hoping for was that we might get through the rest of the summer without killing each other, and it got to be something a lot better than that. When I didn't hardly have a friend in the world, after everything that happened. And I got this idea, and right away I thought, yeah, that's what I should do. I hope I was right."

As she was talking I started letting myself smile, first a little as I walked slowly around the whole thing again, looking up close at the careful lines and etched feather patterns, and by the time I was done I was grinning all the way.

"I can't believe how pretty it is."

I looked around at the bits and pieces of sets and

props, scattered on the floor And—suddenly they didn't look so amateurish and elementary-school anymore. I could almost believe they would be part of something bright and polished and true and real.

"Eee!" Heather squeaked.

"Eee!" I squeaked back, and ran over to her.

"This is going to happen!"

"This is going to happen!"

It wasn't just because of her; it was that this was the first time I had really felt in a good way—not just in a terrified panicky way—that we were going to do this play, that it was really going to work, that nothing would go horribly wrong and we could get to that place where the months of hard work and the splinters and the late nights vanished, and you were left with the raw energy of having created something that didn't exist before. We bounced up and down, and smiled stupidly at each other, and Heather twirled around on the concrete in her socks, and—

It wasn't my idea. I don't think it was hers either—it just happened, my lips against her lips and her hand around my neck.

I heard footsteps upstairs and leaped back, and we stood frozen, staring at each other as if neither one of us had the slightest clue about what to do next.

A door slammed. Someone called out, "I was just leaving, bye!"

I looked at my feet.

"I should go," Heather said. She glanced down at her wrist like she was checking the time, but she didn't have a watch on.

"Are we going to talk about this?"

The corners of her mouth tensed up. "Nothing happened. Forget about it."

"But don't you think—" I forced my voice back down. Even though we were alone. Even if we wouldn't be overheard.

"I finally feel like I have a friend again," Heather continued. "I don't want things to get awkward between us."

"And the way to keep things from getting awkward is to stop talking about them."

Heather looked at me just long enough to show a tight-lipped smile. "We're trying to save Julia's play. And that is what we're going to do. Everything else can wait until we've got that part figured out."

"You're right." I smiled too hard, artificially. But the ground shifted under me. She understood this strange crusade. She fought for it. She made it impossible for me to keep quiet forever about how much I liked her.

THEN

I could not sleep.

It was a better bed than I had had for weeks, except for the few times I'd let myself splurge on a motel, but my mind was whirling too fast for me to do anything but stare up at the ceiling and count very fast sheep. Sheep on methamphetamines.

In the morning, I rode over to Pedal Power to ask about the sign in the window. To see if they wouldn't mind some temporary help, just for a couple of days, so that I could save up a little more money for my rapidly dwindling funds.

The manager was a hippieish-looking guy whose hair had almost faded to white, but remained tied in a short ponytail.

"I'm traveling," I explained, "but I might be hanging around here for a while. That bike out there? I've been from Chicago to here on it. This one hasn't given me too much trouble. I've just had to change flat tires and tighten cables and adjust the derailleurs a little. But my last one was used, and I had to figure out how to fix the brakes, true a wheel, adjust the fit after I grew an inch. And put streamers on the handlebars, of course. I know what I'm doing."

This is how I ended up spending the rest of the afternoon putting bikes together.

That kept my hands busy while leaving my head free to try to work through everything.

I needed the money, if I was going to keep going. No matter how I tried to keep my expenses down, there was only so long I could eat on babysitting money, and I was coming to the end of it too fast. I still had a long way to go, and any number of emergencies might come up between here and California. And there was Maggie, and I didn't want to leave just yet because I liked her, and I wanted to wait just a little and see what happened.

But it made me nervous too. This wasn't part of the plan. I couldn't let myself get off course.

It was just for a day or two. That wouldn't set me back far.

After I was done, I went over to the Market to see Maggie again, and I told her about my new job. "Which is just a temporary thing," I hurried to add. "A couple days."

"All right then," she said tentatively. "Mi futon es su futon."

And that was how things were.

I'd seen the people I knew lose their heads for love before. Lissa acknowledged, when pressed on it, that staring at the back of someone's head was not the most efficient way to tell someone that you liked them, but didn't actually seem able to put it into practice. Jon would drop out of our lives for a week or two at a time and completely lose the ability to talk about anything but the object of his affection. Most of all there was Julia, who had relayed to me every conversation she had with Ollie, so that we could divine whether he liked her or LIKE liked her or what, and so that I could squeal with her. I wanted that with a strange, distant ache— and I didn't want it. Didn't want to act like I'd been hit in the head with a box of bricks, didn't want to stop caring about everything outside our little dyad, didn't want to care that much and hurt that much.

Well. Box of bricks, meet Cassandra. I wish that I could say that I deliberately decided to risk the things I knew weren't wise. That was what I'd said to Maggie, and what I wanted to believe was true. But all it was, was this: For the first time in months I felt *okay*, I no longer felt untethered from the whole world, and I didn't want it to end. Even as I was counting up the days—seven days, eight, nine—and thinking that I must be pushing my schedule, I did not know what else to do.

Everything seemed so new, and everything seemed so temporary, like I had to memorize all that I wouldn't see again. But the ordinary rhythms of one day after another made it seem long, and when the TV shows repeated themselves and I realized a week had passed, I didn't know whether to think that was longer than it seemed or shorter.

The linoleum in the kitchen was cracked and the Laundromat served two-dollar beers on Tuesdays, and it still seemed like fantastic luxury to me. I had long scalding showers every morning. I stayed up late watching bad TV, woke at noon, and didn't get dressed until I had to go to work. Maggie brought ripe peaches from the Market, and purple tomatoes, and big dark grapes, after weeks of energy bars and fast-food value meals. And everywhere I went, I smiled in secret.

I felt decadent and dissolute and bad, and I loved every minute. Of course, it was all ridiculous. I felt all abuzz with mischief and sex and drugs when we were doing nothing more than sneaking cans of PBR and kissing on the futon.

How I loved being ridiculous.

"Silly girl," Maggie said, and ruffled my hair. And I *was* silly. But I couldn't tell her why, couldn't tell her that this was my first time gone head over heels for anyone, my first time out on dates. It was my first time seeing someone's chest rise and fall in a darkened room since Julia had stayed over at my house in March.

I still had the bottle of orange nail polish she'd accidentally left there.

I'd forgotten about that nail polish for weeks. But that Thursday night, when Maggie was working a late shift at the Market, I started digging through my things, looking for it and not finding it, pulling out compartments inside compartments. I had to find it. I could see her, in my mind, bending over my hand and brushing the polish onto my nails. No, that wasn't that last time she'd stayed over at my house—it was other times, when we were younger and not a bit self-conscious, and nail polish was still on that boundary between the things we were allowed and the things that were still just a bit too grown-up. I suddenly felt so far from that person I used to be, and lost, and frightened.

Finally my fingers fastened on to the little glass bottle, so cold and smooth on my skin.

I stared at it for a few moments just to be sure. Then I got some toilet paper from the bathroom, and spread out my fingers, and started carefully painting each nail in turn.

This was something I'd done only a couple of times before, and I always forgot it wasn't as easy as it looked. I kept getting bits of orange on the skin around my fingernails, the tender places I used to nibble when I got nervous. I just managed two slightly messy layers before I got annoyed with the whole thing and decided to make myself a grilled cheese sandwich and check my e-mail on Maggie's laptop.

I didn't expect anything. But there it was, from Oliver, who hadn't sent a word to me in all the weeks I'd been on the road. I stared at it, imagining all the terrible things that could be there, until finally I managed to click on it.

Hi, Cass.

I don't know if you're gonna read this. You're probably still mad at me. You must be in New Mexico by now, right? You haven't updated your journal. We are all wondering about you. Let us know if you're okay?

Hope you come back soon. We should talk.

Ollie.

It was just that little thing. Eight sentences, no grand emotions or dramatic speeches. But I looked away. I shut down the computer. It was something I couldn't face.

I didn't know why he kept trying to get in touch with me, calling me before I left, calling me on the road, this e-mail now. He wasn't sorry about anything, didn't admit that he'd done anything wrong, so what was this? Trying to get an apology out of me, or just a compulsion to pick at wounds that had barely scabbed over?

I wasn't sorry about it anyway.

He didn't have any right to Julia's ashes.

I didn't take them from him. Not exactly. But there was a beginning of a plan, an agreement that whenever Julia's mom decided what to do with her ashes, me and Jon and Oliver would be included in that. When I rode my bike over to her house and told her about what I was going to do, and that I wanted to take Julia's ashes with me, and she said that it was all right—that whole time, I knew exactly what I was taking away from Oliver.

When he found out, he stopped speaking to me at school. And I wasn't even sorry. So how could he write to me like this, carefully emotionless, faking worry?

You must be in New Mexico by now. If I'd kept going, where *would* I be by now? Oklahoma at least, maybe New Mexico, maybe even Arizona and it didn't matter anyway. It was just lines drawn on a map, but it was something bigger than that too. And I had stayed in this town for so many days now promising myself that I would leave.

The door creaked open, and I started. Like I'd been caught doing something wrong.

"I feel like ice cream. There's a good late-night place in the next town over," Maggie announced. "We can drop off our clothes at the Laundromat, go, and get back with enough time to put them in the dryer."

"Sure," I said. I was eager and cheerful and hungry for ice cream—like that dog who was limping over to press her head up against Maggie's pants. But suddenly I felt annoyed with myself, for all the times "Hey, let's—" turned into "Sure" without me thinking it through any further than that.

It's not that she pressured me. Even though she'd said she wasn't going to take responsibility, she treated me like a little young delicate thing. I wasn't sure whether to be offended or reassured by that, so I settled for sleeping chastely nestled in her arms.

I just wanted to be who she wanted me to be, and do what she wanted me to do, because it was better than being miserable and trying not to think about Julia. But I wanted to say no too. Just to prove that I could.

Still, I couldn't say no to ice cream for no good reason, and after already saying yes. So we drove to the next town over, and we got ice cream cones, mint with strawberries and chocolate chips mixed in.

"You painted your nails," Maggie said.

"Yeah." I curled my fingers around—why? It was too late to hide it, or be embarrassed about it, and there was nothing to be embarrassed about anyway. "I mean, I know it's messy, I don't really know how."

"I like the color."

It was not an orange I'd ever have chosen myself, but I liked it too, because Julia was bold enough to wear bright orange nail polish and pull it off. I wanted to remember that about her.

We were quiet as we drove back to the Laundromat.

And when I sat down beside her, watching our clothes spin around in the big dryer, I realized it was the third time I'd been here. That was just because I'd packed light, with as few clothes as I could get away with, and not caring until now if I wore a shirt three days in a row. But still, Oliver had e-mailed me, expecting me to be in New Mexico—

"I probably should get going soon," I said. It didn't mean anything. I'd said it so many times now. It was what I said when I didn't know what to say.

There was a made-for-TV killer-insect movie on the Laundromat TV, and three kids were shrieking at each other chasing around the narrow aisles.

I always started summer vacation with a thousand different passions and ambitions, and then one day I felt like sleeping in, and another day there was something good on TV, and suddenly it would be halfway through August without me having accomplished anything.

I saw what was happening. But I wasn't doing anything about it, and the little squeak of shame inside me somehow made it even harder for me to do anything about it, because I had to look at it before I could do anything.

And I liked it this way.

It wasn't so hard all the time.

"I'm not stopping you," she said, which is what she always said. Kindly, without any judgment in it.

"Yeah, but you're not—"

Before I could finish, she frowned, and drew away from me. I looked around like mad for some way to erase the last minute. The nothing that I'd said was too much. "Never mind."

"Would you be happier if I threw you out or something?"

"I don't know. Maybe." It wasn't what I wanted to say. I could see a scowl pulling at the corners of her lips, I could see her trying not to get angry, or at least not to sound angry.

"I'm not doing anything to keep you here. You can't care that much, you barely know me."

I got up, because I couldn't look at her anymore; I paced to the vending machine and went through my pockets to find enough change for a soda. "I don't know how I can go back to them."

"Them?"

"Look, you don't want to hear the whole stupid story. I got in a fight with some of Julia's friends. Not a big deal."

"How long do you think you can hide out?"

Until Oliver says he's sorry, was what came into my head. Until Lissa or Amy sends me a single word to show they even know who I am. I swallowed it, ashamed. Ashamed too of all the times I'd checked my e-mail hoping for a word from one of them. And now I finally got it, and it wasn't what I wanted to hear, it still wasn't an apology or an admission that Ollie had been wrong, or anything at all that could push us back to being friends again.

I shouldn't want that. I couldn't help wanting it.

"You want to go, fine. You want to stay, fine. But I didn't ask to get mixed up in any he-said, she-said, everybody-hates-me . . ."

"There's a reason I don't tell you about this kind of stuff. I'm trying not to mix you up in it."

We got our clothes folded and drove back home in a grumpy silence.

I didn't go to bed that night. I grabbed a book light and sat down at the flimsy metal card table on the kitchen side of the counter that divided the kitchen off from the rest of the apartment, with my map and my ruler, using a broken pencil to scratch out calculations in the margins. I counted the days I had left before school started, not worrying about the return trip; I could get on a bus when I got to the West Coast. The sixth of August now—that left me with twenty-four days. Counted that against the 1,692 miles I still had left to travel.

More than seventy miles a day.

It was too far. It was way too far, to go across Arizona and New Mexico in the blistering heat (and the wildfires that lit up the whole southwest when we turned on the news). It would be dangerous to try. I'd end up collapsing at the side of the road in some godforsaken desert town, dehydrated, heatstroked.

But what if I went really fast and didn't stop? I've done a hundred miles in a day before.

What if I skipped a week or two of school?

It was a no. It was one of those vast immovable concrete-wall kind of nos. Not just a no from the real world and the laws of physics, but a no from deep down inside me: *I can't do this. I'm not strong enough. I have stayed here instead of going forward because I am weak, and scared, and useless, and there's no point to this anymore.*

A great mass of grief rose up in my throat at the unfairness of the world. It didn't seem right that I could go so far and try so hard and fail like this. If I could have a noble failure, that would be different; there wasn't anything noble about being lazy and scared and infatuated. And if I tried to go on now anyway, it would be for nothing.

I felt so childish and small, that I had tried to do this thing that everyone else said I'd never be able to do, and it turned out that they were right. I wasn't any different from a seven-year-old kid, outraged at her family, who runs away from home and makes it all of three or four blocks before turning back. They'll all be sorry when I'm gone, I'd been thinking, just like that kid I used to be—and still was.

This was different, though; this was a betrayal.

I had loved Julia so much.

I had gone across five hundred miles and two states trying to understand that and figure it out and remember her and pay tribute to her and somehow, somehow, share these days and these nights with her. And in the

197

end I had betrayed her. I'd chickened out and chosen laziness and selfishness and I'd abandoned her.

She was dead anyway. It couldn't make that much difference to her whether I abandoned her or betrayed her or attempted some futile quest of a road-trip for her sake.

It didn't matter, because she was dead.

It had never hit me like that before: that it was absurd to dedicate myself to a dead girl. That I had tried anyway, and failed.

That she was dead.

I laid my head on my arms, with the metal of the table pressing hard against my elbows, and sobbed and sobbed until I couldn't possibly have any more sadness in me, but it kept on rolling over me in waves that knocked me over as soon as I thought I could breathe again.

That's how Maggie found me when she got up the next morning. Exhausted, hot, nauseous with tears.

The next thing I knew, I was picking up the clothes I'd left on the floor and throwing my things together into my panniers, without bothering to be neat about anything.

I was talking without knowing what I was saying, not listening to my own words.

"I should've been gone a long time ago, instead of just letting my time slip away from me."

"Nobody's ever kept you here except yourself." There was ice in her voice; I couldn't bear to listen to her. "This was a bad idea from the start."

"Yeah, but it was your bad idea too." I shouldered past her as I went to gather my toothbrush from the bathroom. There was no room in here, everything was too close. I couldn't get away. And I still had to get my notebook, my granola bars, my purple T-shirt that was lying on the floor—

"And I took responsibility for that part, so maybe you could do the same thing. What have I ever been to you, anyway, other than a distraction from your stupid dead girlfriend, while you waited for your friends to come around and realize how horribly they wronged you?"

"Don't even," I said. "Don't even start, when you don't understand any of this."

So she left, slamming the door behind her. Then, from behind the door, she yelled, "I'm not going to stand out here in the rain forever, so if you want to grab your stuff and leave, just do it."

I tried to cram everything I had into my panniers. It didn't work very well, because I didn't bother to fold anything, and I ended up letting them overflow and carried the rest in my arms to where my bike was locked under the metal stairs. I tried not to look at her.

I repacked my panniers and managed to get everything in there this time. I felt the bottle of orange nail polish in my hand again, hard, cold. It was drizzling and cool as I rode my bike toward the edge of town, the sun lurking pale and distant behind clouds.

We had only a week left before the premiere. If I came in at seven to work on putting things together before school, there were always a few other people who'd come in early too; and if it was already getting dark when I left, there were always a few other people staying later. Other times I'd worked on helping out with the sets, people slacked off, joked around, pretended to get work done. This time there wasn't any pretending, except when we strenuously denied the existence of *Totally Sweet Ninja Death Squad*.

The worst part was the lights, because I did not like high

places, and I did not trust electricity. I knew enough that I would not do something silly to get myself electrocuted—but still, I was never quite sure that if I did everything right, the electricity would keep its end of the bargain.

Thursday afternoon, after school, I'd been up there for the better part of an hour, and was starting to get shaky on my feet, but I had that maniacal intensity of purpose that wouldn't let me take a break just yet. I told myself I'd just keep going a few more minutes, just set up one more light. And then—when I was up on the ladder with maybe eight feet between my shoes and the ground, one of the lights cut out. I started poking at it, and gingerly started to unscrew it from its socket, when a spark flew out and flashed in my eyes.

A second later I was holding on to the ladder so tightly that my fingers hurt from pressing into the metal edges, and breathing in and out very carefully, as if one wrong move would be enough to send me toppling down.

I didn't look down when Heather called up to me, "Are you okay?"

"I'm fine. I got spooked, that's all." It felt like a very, very long way down.

"Take a break. It's going to start getting dark soon, and Lissa brought us some snacks."

"Okay," I said. And then, trying to take a step down, my legs froze into place. I couldn't get myself to move.

I stayed there at the top of the ladder, willing myself to get over it and come down.

"I'm not fine," I managed to say. "I'm scared up here."

The ladder wobbled a little. I drew in a frightened breath, and then heard Heather's voice from below. "I've got the ladder. My hands are just under where your feet are. Take one step down. I'll make sure you don't fall."

Forcing myself to breathe slowly, I lifted one foot off the step, and it hung in the air for a too-long minute.

"Right below you. About a half inch more."

I stretched my leg just a little farther down, until miraculously I felt the hard ridged steel under my sole.

"There you go. You're okay there."

She talked me down four steps that way, and each time I was a little less terrified to look below me, and finally I let go of the frame of the ladder and grabbed on to her outstretched hand so that I could come down the rest of the way.

Back on solid ground, I burst into the anxious laughter that comes from deep in human history when it meant Ha! False alarm, that's not a bear coming to eat us, you can stop panicking now.

"Your hand," Heather said. I looked down. Where the edges of the ladder had bit into my hand, sharp lines of blood were limned across my palm, crossing the faint lines left from the first time I'd cut myself in her presence; and Heather's hand was touched with red too.

I sighed as I went to the first aid cabinet. "I'm not so fond of heights."

"I know," Heather said, and it took me a few moments to remember how she could have known that.

In seventh-grade gym class—it rained that day, so we were rotating in small groups through various activities in the gym, mostly unsupervised. And as I was most of the way to the top of the climbing rope, Heather and one of her friends decided that it would be hilarious to start swinging the rope below me. I couldn't get down. And I stayed there, hanging on desperately to the knots under my hands and feet, until class ended and the coach chewed me out because he hadn't seen me at any of the other activities I was supposed to be doing, and all of this had passed beneath his notice.

I laughed awkwardly again. "I'd forgotten about that."

"I didn't."

She sat down on one of the rubber-covered stepstools scattered around the dim mess backstage, looking away from me, and by the time I sat down beside her I'd made up my mind.

"Heather—look, I'm not saying it's okay, because it's not, all right? But that's not what I think about when I think about you anymore."

"What do you think about, then?"

"You kissed me."

That made her look at me, finally. Her face flushed a little. "I didn't mean to."

"I don't expect you to still be pining over someone you used to like way back when—God, when you liked the Backstreet Boys—but I just wanted to say it. Because it's true."

"Not pining," she admitted. "But I look at you and you're so . . . awkward, and scruffy, and fearless, and just intensely yourself, and I remember why I fell so hard for you. And in another universe, who knows?"

I reached out and put my hand lightly over hers, and she let it stay there just for a moment before she pulled away.

"But in *this* universe it's not a good idea."

"Because of the play? We've only got a week to the premiere."

"Not because of that." She chewed on her lip. She seemed to be searching for words that weren't there to be found. "Because, to you, I'm always going to be that girl you couldn't stand, ever since third grade."

"It's not like that."

"But it will be like that, when I screw up and act like a total bitch, when you realize that I haven't changed as much as you wanted."

"You don't know that."

She shook her head. "I was scribbling your name in my notebook and then blacking it out with Magic Marker, and I was so sure that you were fine, you were okay, you didn't have problems like I did, and I sort of hated you for it. But the you who is in my heart and in my memory, who I had a ridiculous crush on, who

I'm still a bit angry at, never really existed in the first place. It's got nothing to do with the real you. So—" She smiled regretfully. "You can tell I've thought about this way too much trying to pretend it's not a bad idea."

"What's so bad about a bad idea? Sometimes those can turn out all right in the end."

Everything I'd done since Julia died had been a bad idea. All of it from the beginning to this moment. And I didn't know if I would take it back, or if I wouldn't, if I had the choice—but it was a path that had led me, wandering and lurching in the dark, to here. That was all right with me.

"And sometimes they don't. I'm not ready to step into another heartbreak with my eyes wide open. I've been through that already." She let out a long breath, not completely hopeless. "I need to think about this. Not that I haven't thought about this already, but I need to think about this."

"You're probably right," I murmured, even though she wasn't. She was wrong. But I didn't want to fight with her, didn't want to press her into a corner if she was just trying to be nice. So I tried to smile, which didn't work that well, and we started to clean up—we were meticulous about that, trying to avoid raising any suspicions about how late we were at the theater.

Inside, I was wincing. I hadn't been expecting more, no; but I'd been hoping, without even realizing it, hoping that she would be surprised and gleeful and ready to kiss me again. And that was totally unreasonable, but I hoped anyway.

She offered me a ride that evening, like usual.

I rode home by myself.

Then on Sunday night as I was about to go to bed, with my pajamas on and my hair damp from a shower, I heard a ping at my window—and then another one. I looked down, and there was Heather. And an instrument case, and the kind of flashlight with a clamp and a snaky neck, and the moonlight shining round and white on her hair.

I opened the window and crossed my arms on the windowsill and leaned my head out while Heather set up all her things, her chair and her music stand and her score. She didn't look up at me, and I didn't call down to her. I didn't want to disturb the spell that seemed to be upon us.

She lifted her clarinet up to her lips and played a long, low, reedy note.

I didn't know about music in any kind of intellectual way. And Heather had told me before that she only played the clarinet badly.

But it was beautiful. Graceful and soft and melancholy. She tripped on a note once in a while, but it wasn't a fast melody, and she always picked it up as if nothing had happened.

She showed me the night air and the moon, and the delicate precision in her slender fingers, and the controlled intensity of her breath, and I loved all of it.

No one had ever played music just for me before, and all I could do was enjoy it, disconcerting as it was. But when the music stopped, and I waited, she didn't look up at me.

"Heather," I called from my window. But still she didn't look up. She got on with putting away her clarinet, and her music stand, and her flashlight, and her chair, efficient and businesslike as if she didn't know I was up there only half breathing.

I went to bed telling myself, I will not, will not, will not pick over this with my brain, not when I'm going to see Heather in first period tomorrow. I will not.

So I tried to get to sleep—and picked over it with my brain until, an hour later, I remembered that I'd sworn not to do that. And so on until both me and my brain were mercifully too exhausted to do anything more.

THEN

I turned over in my head
what to do next, not pedaling to get anywhere but just
to give myself something to do. I had stayed for twelve
days. I had a hundred and eighty dollars from working at Pedal Power and a little more left over from my
babysitting money.

I would not make it across Oklahoma and Texas and
Arizona and New Mexico and California in the time
that I had left. Even if I tried, it would only be stupid
and dangerous. The sensible thing was to figure out
where was the nearest place I could get on a Greyhound

pointed in the direction of home. It probably would be less than one eighty for the ticket and food, and that way I wouldn't have to talk to my parents about everything that had gone wrong. I would be able to pretend that everything was okay.

I didn't do that.

The hard-coiled stubborn thing inside me said *no*, and I didn't have the energy to argue.

I started pedaling, hard. So hard I could feel it in muscles and skin and bone, hot, painful. I burned from nothing and into nothing. I didn't have a place to go anymore, I didn't have a reason to go anymore—because I had betrayed all that—and I knew I wouldn't get there. I'd be more likely to roast under the desert sun. So there was nothing except just to keep going forward, as long as there was any forward to go to.

I didn't check my maps. I forgot all the usual advice: Drink before you're thirsty, eat before you're hungry, stop before you're tired. I didn't drink, didn't eat, didn't stop. I had become a spark of aimless and unstoppable determination.

Stretching legs that hadn't really been stretched in nearly two weeks, not bothering to pace myself, I just pedaled. Legs up and down, forward and back, remembering the feel of water against my face, and the speed of the wind through my hair, and what it was like to fly so fast under no power but the strength of my own limbs. I felt my mind go blank, and my heart as well, and there was no need anymore to think or grieve or blame myself or anyone else. There was just existence, and survival, and speed.

Half an hour out, it seemed that the world was well and truly deserted, and I managed to hide myself inside a copse of trees and change my clothes. My jeans were biting at me from half a dozen different angles, and the skin inside my thighs had been rubbed red and raw. I didn't notice until then that I wasn't wearing my helmet—I buckled it on and tried not to flash back to the dire warnings of what will happen to your head if you don't wear one. Now that I finally had a chance to catch my breath, my hunger and my melancholy rose up over me like a shroud.

I drank down all the water that I had left and kept going.

The hunger and fatigue came over me gradually. I hadn't slept, hadn't eaten since the ice cream the night before. The whole world started to seem dim and strange, as if I was traveling through a postapocalyptic landscape where there were no people at all, and I could only keep going until I died of thirst; or maybe I wouldn't even be able to die, and I would just keep going on forever by myself, alone in a wasteland.

Finally, somehow, I found a decrepit gas station that charged me a ridiculous sum for three bottles of water, a bag of nuts, and a suspicious sandwich, which I wolfed down—it actually tasted slightly better than it looked—before starting back on my way.

When I collapsed, exhausted, with the bloody red of the setting sun in my eyes, I hardly knew where I was or where I'd been or how long I'd been going. There was a dull ache in my legs and my back that told me I'd probably done more than I should have, and that I'd regret it in the morning. Around me was a patchwork of fields, no different from what I'd been riding through all day, though a little more brown and yellow, and less green.

As I crawled into my tent, I was thinking about how dumb I'd been, how I was probably lost now, how I'd barely be able to move in the morning. But sleep fell over me before I had time to think about that.

I woke up with stiff muscles complaining in my legs and back and arms and neck. But I still had nothing in my mind except to just keep going and keep going and keep going, and I did, taking the sun as my guide and not bothering to figure out where I was until I finally limped into Tulsa. On the map, it didn't look like a huge distance, but I'd covered a hundred and sixty miles in the space of two days. Far too much for my body to handle.

It meant that if I could just keep going like this, then I would make it after all. Distance equals velocity times time; I kept adjusting the time (I could spend more hours on the road, I could skip the break in the hottest part of the day) and the velocity (I could go faster. I could just make myself go faster). And it maybe, almost, barely worked out. I didn't know whether that gave me hope or despair, and I tried not to think too much about the implications.

I was starving, and thirsty, and I thought that I would fall apart if I had to walk another step farther. So I checked myself into the first motel I found, and didn't even bother to get my packs off my bike before I went up to my room and fell into bed. There was still a part of my heart that winced whenever I poked at it, and whenever I stopped for long enough to catch my breath, I started poking again. I kept telling myself that things would look better in the morning, and then rolling over to try once more to go to sleep.

Things did look better in the morning, kind of. I had air-conditioning, for one thing, and a clean blanket, and the sun streaming in through the plastic blinds, and inane morning chatter on the TV.

I gorged myself on bacon and pancakes in the motel restaurant, and then I went out around the back to get my bike.

Huh, that's weird, I thought at first. I thought for sure that's where I parked it. Behind the hotel where it wasn't in sight of everyone who might come wandering by, securely affixed to the metal stairs. But then, I wasn't thinking all that clearly the night before. If I was thinking, I would've brought some of my stuff inside instead of leaving it all on packs on the bike. Maybe I locked it somewhere else and forgot.

I walked the perimeter of the property, casting my eyes everywhere, toward trees and lampposts and anything that looked solid enough to lock something to.

I walked it twice. A bike doesn't walk off just by itself, and it's too big to lose, and even if I hadn't been smart enough to lock up my panniers I did lock my bike with a four-star lock, guaranteed against theft in sixteen states.

Finally something caught my eye, lying balefully in the grass: I picked up a sawed-through piece of a bike lock.

I didn't want to believe that it could be mine. But I had to be sure, so I took out my key and slid it into the keyhole.

It turned. The broken pieces of the lock fell apart into the grass.

As I started to get my head around the impossible—my bike was gone, stolen—I tried to work things through in my head. At first I had trouble thinking anything but Ohgodno, Ohgodno, Ohgodno, Ohgodno, and then various chains of thoughts started to float up to the surface.

1) What I no longer had. For example: all my clothing. My transportation. My camping equipment. Nearly all my money.

2) What I still had. The clothing I had on me, a credit card for emergencies plus ten dollars that I kept stuffed between my sock and my

shoe, and the cell phone in my pocket. I didn't even have the charger. Two days was about the most I could expect to get from my phone.

3) What I couldn't bear to think about. Julia's ashes. The things I had been collecting for her.

But who on earth would steal two plastic boxes containing absolutely nothing useful? A handful of weeds and feathers and roadside debris, and ashes? They had to still be around here somewhere. Unless the thief had left without checking the panniers—but that didn't make any sense, they were too heavy.

I forgot, for the moment, about figuring out food, or shelter, or transportation; I was still locked into a state of panic. In that moment, nothing at all seemed as important as finding Julia's things—it was too big to deal with all at once, so all I could do was chew at the nearest corner. I set myself to walking in loose concentric circles in the brush around the motel. Time and again, something glinted at me, and I realized that it was only a bit of trash, a food wrapper.

And then, finally, something made me draw in my breath and try not to hope. Two clear boxes, dumped carelessly on the grass. But the lips had stayed firmly sealed; everything was there. Everything was fine. I counted my treasures; I counted them again. I wouldn't have known exactly how many there were supposed to be, but I had my feather, and my Hot Wheels car, and my grimy little action figure, and my bit of candle, and all of a sudden I was okay. I was okay, even though I had no money and no transportation and no clothing that I wasn't wearing.

I let out one great sigh of relief that started me crying again, this time in stifled little sniffles. I had checked out of my room already. I didn't have a place to have a nervous breakdown, or the luxury of being able to cry. All I could do was blink at my tears.

The best and the worst part of it all was that I knew exactly what I was going to do, because there weren't any other options. I wasn't going to get far on ten dollars—and the credit card was so that I could have some alternative to being homeless and stranded if worst should come to worst, not so that I could have a happy fun summer vacation on my parents' dime. That left the bus, and the train.

A dignified defeat, at least. I could charge the trip, and pay them back later—and of course I would have to call my parents, to explain what was going on.

I got to the bus depot in little spurts, stopping strangers on the street for directions. There I was, a teenage girl, no possessions, looking for a bus to get out of here, looking like a runaway or an addict for the anxiety on my face and the way I looked like I hadn't slept in years. I saw people turn away when I tried to approach. Not that I could blame them.

The bus depot depressed me. Sticky concrete on the floor, patches of old dried gum, families huddled together. A pair of kids fighting over whose turn it was to play the Game Boy. I started hunting around for schedules, and as I was standing there, not really waiting in any particular line, a woman in a bus uniform came up and asked me if I needed help.

"No," I said. And then "Yes," and then "No" again.

I couldn't handle it. I felt bent and broken; this me who was bravely going to the bus station and being very independent and mature wasn't real. It was crumbling from under me and now I was emptied out. I didn't have the strength to get home, and I didn't have the strength to ask for help.

I went outside and tried to keep myself from crying, wiping my eyes over and over until I thought I could speak again.

I took the cell phone out of my pocket to call Mom. No. My pride was too much. Before I had decided to, I was dialing Ollie's number.

"Cassie," he said as he picked up. "I haven't heard a word from you in, like, forever. I was starting to wonder if you were dead."

"No," I said quietly. "Not dead yet."

"So that's something, then." I could just about hear his nervous smile. The way he was trying to ignore anything that had ever happened between us.

"You can say no to what I'm going to ask you," I said.

"It's okay, because I can still call my parents, and I can still get a bus ticket, and it's really—I guess we're not good enough friends for me to impose on you like this."

"I haven't said no yet."

I stayed quiet for a while, choking down my nervousness. "My bike's gone. Somebody sawed through the lock."

Silence, for long enough that I worried that my phone had dropped the call. "That thing's worth more than my car!"

"And I . . . It's not like I don't have any other way to get home, Ollie. But I don't know how to keep going on by myself. I need somebody to not say I told you so."

"Where are you?"

"It's not New Mexico," I said. "Stuff happened."

"Where are you?"

"Tulsa. Oklahoma."

"Damn, that's kind of awesome." He laughed, without any humor in it. "That's . . . a lot."

"I know, it's too far. I'll figure out something else."

"Cassie, wait," he said.

I waited.

"Don't figure out something else, not yet. Just—can you sit tight where you are without being totally homeless?"

"I can put a motel room on my credit card."

"Okay. Well. We're so far behind schedule on *Totally Sweet Ninja Death Squad*, a few days more won't make

217

a difference. Stay put, I'll be there when I can."

My throat was too tight for me to speak. I hung up, and then, because I figured my parents would be at work, I called home and left a message on the machine saying not to worry, because I was okay, and I was having a bit of an emergency but it was already being resolved. That's it. I couldn't tell them anything else, not yet.

I found a used bookstore and bought a mystery novel with my ten-dollar bill; I spent most of the rest of the day reading it in one spot or another, wandering around whenever I got restless or too self-conscious. In the evening, I checked back into my motel, and at some point I drifted off to sleep.

The tinny ringing of "Für Elise" from my cell phone woke me up. I blinked, staring at the clock radio: 2:14. In the morning.

I fumbled for the phone, not really awake enough to check the caller ID or realize why anyone would be calling me.

"What?"

"Where in Tulsa?"

I finally managed to get my brain working right for long enough to give Ollie directions.

"Check out and wait outside. I'll be by in a sec." I heard weary impatience, frustration, and I was cringing on the inside by the time I got down. Looking at the red-eyed guy at the desk who checked me out, I felt like the whole world had decided to be mad at me.

I sat down on the steps outside, perking up at every headlight that flashed by, and then suddenly one turned into the parking lot, and blared a horn.

Oliver's Buick was ancient, and humongous, and cared for with meticulous precision—it was how the three of us always got to school in the rain, even after Julia had her own car. I would've known it anywhere. Only—I didn't expect there to be anyone in it but him. And yet the back door opened, and Amy came out, and pushed me into the middle backseat. It was the only seat still open.

Lissa was driving, and Ollie was in the front seat beside her. Amy and Jon sandwiched me in the backseat.

It was almost three a.m., and there wasn't a chorus of squealing and hellos and what's going ons. It was just Jon and Amy on either side of me, quiet, with their shoulders up against mine. And Jon reached over and put his hand over mine; and then Amy did too.

"We've been driving shifts," Amy said in a whisper. "Eleven hours. We only went *kind of* over the speed limit, not really really over."

"Thank you," I said. Like that would cover it. Like it would come anywhere close to covering it. But what else was there to say, at three in the morning?

I sat there in the darkness, with their skin close to me, and I felt lifted up and wrapped with kindness. And very small, because I didn't at all deserve this, but small the way a mouse in its den is small: warm and safe and protected.

NOW

In the morning I was in the garage, putting air in my tires, when Heather's car rolled by and honked at me. I climbed in without a second thought and put my face up to the air vent blowing cold air at me. Even the recycled air felt good on such a gray, humid, muggy morning, the kind of morning that would've had me rushing to the bathroom before class to brush out my hair and towel off sweat.

And then I felt Heather staring at me.

"What was that?" I asked. "Last night—"

"Brahms, Intermezzo. It's what you want to play if

you're not much good, because it sounds a lot more impressive than it actually is. And also, it's not very fast, which is good because I've hardly picked up my clarinet in the last year. It's surprising how muscle memory sticks with you. Okay. Shutting up now."

She spent a few minutes fiddling with the air-conditioning, the radio, and finally started driving.

"So I said I was going to think about this. And what I thought, in the end, was that for so long I just wanted a do-over with you. A second chance to start sixth grade by walking over to your table in the cafeteria and asking if I could sit down. And I got it, somehow, and I don't know how or why, but if I throw away this chance I know I won't get another one. And that's not acceptable to me. So—I hope you're not mad that I had to think about it, and that I'm making myself be a little bit logical. It's not romantic. But stupidity never did anybody any favors."

"It's okay," I said. I *liked* logic, and there was something sweet in her carefulness. "I don't think I could ask for anything better than music outside my window in the middle of the night."

We pulled into an empty parking lot. The dashboard clock said 7:03, twenty-seven minutes before first period.

The sun had risen, but the sky still had the pale, deathly color of too-early-in-the-morning. Heather stretched out, slung her purple backpack over one shoulder, and grabbed my hand as we walked inside.

"Library?"

"Library," Heather answered. I moved half a step behind her, acutely aware all of a sudden both of the warmth of her hand and the emptiness of the hallways. But shadows roamed here and there, the teachers and athletes and the band people who came early and stayed late, and their footsteps nearly made me jump out of my skin.

Even though there was no reason to be secretive.

What, I was going to surprise the three percent of the school who hadn't already decided I was gay? I was going to hear snide comments from the people who already considered me fair game for snide comments? I'd had time to get used to this.

So it was okay. It had me on my toes, but it was definitely okay.

Watching Heather, I wondered if the same thing was going through her head. This had to be new for her too, but she seemed so certain. How long had she been waiting, to be able to hold someone's hand in the hallway?

She ducked her head into the library, glanced here and there, and paced purposefully through the shelves. Slow and graceful, like she was in character as a ninja princess even now.

She turned a corner and we were in a nook where no one could see us. Books on two sides, and a vast picture window overlooking the swampy creek side where kids would go to smoke pot at lunch.

She bent over the books, running her hands over the

spines, and I crouched down to see what she was looking at.

She was looking at me.

I glanced away, because I was anxious and because I was looking for a book—one that should be right there—and then she leaned in and kissed me. On my neck, just below my ear. I breathed in the smell of her hair, lemon and rosewood, sweet and dark.

Wow.

My anxiety and bewilderment and confusion blew out of my head and there was nothing but that wow, her smell, and the touch of her skin on my skin.

And she smiled just a little, and looked away, and picked a paperback from the shelf.

"This one, I think. No?"

"No. This one." A dull green book, perhaps forty years old and beaten by the years. At one time or another I'd read most of the dating advice books in the library, trying to figure out what I was missing. Judging by this one, I wasn't missing much.

She glanced at the cover, opened to a random page. And started reading it to me, until she cracked up halfway through and handed it to me. "According to this, I'm not a girl."

"Yeah, me neither. So that makes us . . ."

"Gay men?"

As we were giggling, a girl showed up around the corner with a cart of books and gave us a withering stare.

I put my head down like I'd been caught in the middle of something wrong, but Heather just smiled back, all demure innocence, and started toward the door. Inwardly I marveled: This was a girl who'd survived three years of Catholic school. How had she learned to be many things at once, and not let it break her?

Heather had passed notes to me in English class since the start of the school year, to make fun of nearly everything we were studying—not like most of my classmates who thought that novels and poetry were stupid by definition, but like her standards were way too high for this class.

That morning she passed me a tiny triangle of paper, elaborately folded in some pattern I couldn't fathom, and I started unfolding it under my desk.

"Miss Meyer," Dr. Vesper said. He was a small and elderly man who sometimes looked like he was about to die, and sometimes looked like he already had. "Would you care to share that with the rest of the class?"

I looked at the poem in my hand, which I hadn't even had a chance to read yet, and said, "Actually, I would."

And I stood up and started to read aloud, hoping desperately that it wasn't anything we'd both get in trouble for. I looked to Heather for help, but she just had her hand over her face and an expression somewhere between horror and embarrassment and delight.

"You are the bread and the knife,
the crystal goblet and the wine.
You are the dew on the morning grass
and the burning wheel of the sun.
You are the white apron of the baker,
and the marsh birds suddenly in flight.

"However, you are not the wind in the orchard,
the plums on the counter,
or the house of cards.
And you are certainly not the pine-scented air.
There is just no way that you are the pine-scented air."

I got to this point and stopped reading. I wanted to sit down. It was too much for me to take in.

"Would you care to *explain* this, Miss Meyer?"

I shook my head, because I couldn't explain it, and I felt stupid because I couldn't explain it. But I didn't need to explain it; I just wanted to listen to it right now, and read it over in my head. I slid back into my seat.

"Anyone else?"

Heather had stuck her hand up into the air and was waving it around like a little kid who really, really wanted to get called on.

"Miss Galloway?"

I didn't want her to explain it. Not now. I wanted to go back into the library and sit in front of the picture window and listen, there, to what she had to say.

"Poems are not for explaining," she said, her tone as bored and faintly scornful as his. "They are for pretty girls to read aloud. Everyone knows that. Can we get back to Hawthorne now?"

And we did—but I spent that period and the next one letting those words tumble around in my head, still dazed at the thought that the words were for me.

"Billy Collins," she said at lunchtime. For a change we didn't sit over by Jon and Ollie and the others, but on the other side of the campus, perched on tall boulders with one flat stone between us for our thermoses and sandwiches.

"I don't think I really got it," I said. I had read it three times all the way through by then. "But it was interesting."

"I wasn't being facetious or anything, what I said before. Poems aren't for understanding or explaining, not if they're any good."

That was good enough for me.

And really, everything in all the world was good enough for me until after the end of eighth period, at my locker, when I was sorting through my books to figure out which ones I needed for homework and which ones I could leave at school—and I noticed Gwen standing there.

Gwen had always picked on me with utter apathy. Like, if she couldn't find any of her friends to gossip with, and if her boyfriend wasn't around, and if she didn't have any interesting plans for the day, she might go find me out of force of habit and see if I was having a bad hair day.

So I saw her there, and I didn't see her. And really, it didn't matter. What was gonna bring me down today?

"You really didn't waste any time, did you?"

I didn't know what she was talking about. Didn't care either. I turned back to my locker, pretending to look in my assignment book.

She took a step closer to me and pointedly looked inside—at the pictures stuck in the door, with me and Julia waving at the camera from a Ferris wheel, the two of us in our bathing suits at the water park, Julia in her prom dress after we'd gone shopping for it—that one was the last picture I had from before she died. The accident was just a couple weeks before prom, and I had had to call and cancel the limo because Ollie couldn't do it.

"I mean, it makes sense. When you've got a straight girl to pine for, you shut up and pretend that you don't, and now that she's gone you can finally get a life. But you sure didn't wait for her corpse to cool."

I bit down on my lip so hard it hurt. Not that I was biting back words—but hearing it made my face tense up, violently.

"What the hell makes it your business?"

"Everyone is going to think it's their business. You should know that."

"What do you want me to do, announce it over the PA system?"

She shrugged. "I'm just saying."

She walked off. Mission accomplished. It hit me in the gut.

Didn't wait for her corpse to cool.

God.

I'd been through this. I wasn't being disloyal to a dead straight girl who'd never so much as kissed my forehead.

But when the environmental science teacher drew a smiley face on my essay, when I tried to stand up for myself in military history, I wasn't thinking anymore, *I wish Julia could still be around to see this, I wish I could tell her*. I was thinking that I wanted to tell Heather.

So Gwen was right, or she was wrong, and I didn't know, and it didn't matter. It didn't change the shame, and the hurt.

I stood in the hallway, tilting my head at the ceiling so I could blink back the tears in my eyes.

"Something interesting up there?"

Heather was leaning against the locker beside mine. I didn't know how much time had passed; the corridor had mostly emptied out.

"Hey. What's up?" She half smiled. "So to speak."

"Nothing. It's no big deal."

"Don't give me that." She brushed her thumb along the line of my cheek and my jaw. "I know that somebody-was-mean-to-me face."

"Well, it's not a big deal if somebody was mean to me. It shouldn't be a big deal."

"Yeah, and maybe I should have been all gay-pride in front of the nuns, but I wasn't, was I? Should's got nothing to do with it."

"I don't care if people think I'm gay. That's no different from every year since sixth grade."

"What is it, then?"

Julia. It was Julia. But no, I wasn't about to tell her that, I wasn't about to put that out there where she could use it against me. "I just, I'm starting to think you're right. It's not a good idea."

Heather put her hand over my shoulder, and tugged me toward her. "Don't let them get to you. I know you, you're stronger than that."

I jerked away from her. "How do you get the right to say that? To be the one who sticks up for me and pats me on the shoulder? You were on *their* side."

She stared at me, speechless. As soon as it was out of my mouth I wished I could take it back, I wished it wasn't there in the air between us holding the moment frozen.

"I knew you couldn't get over it," she said. "Why do you think I said it was a bad idea? Why do you think I kept quiet when I realized I had as much of a crush on you as I ever did?"

"I didn't mean it!"

Heather turned away from me. As she talked, she clipped her words short, pruned the emotions from her voice.

"Of course you meant it. You're going to deny it,

because you want to keep thinking that you're honorable and forgiving and peaceful, and—you've got stupid petty resentments and grudges like everybody else. So you might as well admit it."

"I can admit it. I *have* admitted it. But that's not what this is about."

I stood there shaking my head, why won't you listen to me, why won't you let me try to fix this?

"Go ahead. Tell me that you trust me, at all."

And I—I just couldn't get myself to say anything.

It wasn't distrust. It was a different thing, a hard cold thing that I couldn't grasp and didn't want to grasp.

"Obviously I couldn't just be sensible for once. Obviously I'd have to go and get my heart broken twice in a year. But I thought maybe it'd be different with you."

"Just— Just let me—"

"Okay."

Her face softened, her hands went up. "Talk."

She stayed like that, silent, for longer than I deserved. Long enough to force me to try to wrestle my thoughts into submission.

It was about that dead girl I wasn't being disloyal to.

I wished I could have told her that. And I tried to, tried to find someplace I could start, but there wasn't any good place.

In the end I gave up. "Forget it."

Heather stepped back, her head hanging down. "Cass, don't do this to me."

"Seriously, forget it. You're right. You win."

She shoved her hands in her pockets, started to walk away, and turned back again. "You're not walking home, are you?"

"Yeah. I am."

THEN

There was nothing in the world I loved so much as traveling home at night. It felt like there was something waiting for me, warm and reassuring, and it felt like now I had already passed through all the challenges and the hard things, and I could get there if I just waited quietly in the dark and the calm. I fell asleep like that, and when I woke up, the drivers had changed; Amy now. Lissa was sleeping beside me.

I said "Thank you" again, because Ollie was awake now.

"Someday you will owe us a story worthy of eleven

hours in an old Buick," he said. "But today is not that day. Mostly because none of us are very awake. Oh, and say thank you to Lissa too, when she wakes up. We ended up going to this terrible burger place where they fried their fries in beef fat, and when she asked for whatever they had that was vegetarian they gave her a melted piece of cheese on a hamburger bun. And while we're eating, her *grandmère* calls, and she has to *lie* because she doesn't want a lecture about how her *grandmère* didn't spend all that time teaching her to cook just so she could be eating a piece of cheese on a hamburger bun."

"I don't have a story worthy of all this," I said. "Not yet. But I think maybe I have a little one."

I thought I only had a little one, it's true, but once I'd started talking, the words spilled out of me, and I told them everything of what had happened from the day I'd left to the days I'd spent with Maggie to having my bike and everything on it stolen.

"And so all I've got left is these two boxes. One is all the stuff that I've picked up because it reminded me of Julia, or because I thought she would like it, or—I don't know. And the other has Julia's ashes."

Which sent a collective shiver through the whole car, and then, just silence.

Oliver, from the front passenger seat, looked back at me. "I'm not going to get upset by whatever you say, or if you don't say anything, but . . . were you in love with Julia?"

"Come on, Ollie," Jon said. "That's a hell of a question to answer before dawn when you've just had your heart broken and your bike stolen."

"Objection sustained."

Yeah. It was a hell of a question.

"I don't even know if I'm gay."

"Still? After all this?"

"It's one girl," I said. "How am I supposed to know whether I like girls in general, or only girls, or this one girl who rescued me from a flash flood? One is a terrible sample size to get any meaningful data from."

I smiled. "I wish I could be sure. That would be so much simpler."

The sky was starting to lighten, barely, almost imperceptibly. It was the kind of liminal hour when almost anything might be possible. Even putting into words what I'd never been able to put into words before.

"So, look . . ." I said. "When I set out on this trip I thought I was going to California on my bike. And the idea is, if you just keep going west and manage not to get squashed by an eighteen-wheeler, that's where you're going to end up. But if it was just about getting to California I could have saved myself a lot of heartache and bought a plane ticket. And I wouldn't be in the middle of nowhere with you guys right now."

"You didn't know."

"I could've known, if I'd thought about it for three seconds. I could have guessed that I wasn't getting to

California. I should have known that things were going to go all off the way I planned them. But just at the same time things are going wrong, things are going right too, like infatuation and working for an old hippie bike mechanic and having friends who will drive all the way from Chicago in a night. Maybe not following the plan I'd set out for myself was the best thing that I could've done. So I'm not going to California. That's fine. I'm going where I'm supposed to be, even when I don't know where that is. And me being gay, or not, or whatever, it's like that. I'll get to where I need to go, even if right now I have no idea of where that is."

"Cass," Jon said, a restrained grin tugging up the corners of his mouth.

"Yeah?"

"I got news for you." He motioned backward, and I looked out the rear windshield, at the pale ball half submerged on the horizon.

Yeah, so the sun's rising. Behind us.

It took me a while to figure it out. I hadn't slept enough, couldn't think through the implications well enough. If the sun rose behind us . . .

We were going west.

I called out, "We're going the wrong way."

"Are not," Amy said.

"We thought about it and we took a vote," Ollie said. "We aren't going to let any jackass bike thief get in the way of your mission."

It hit me with a weight that can't be put into words: I had the best friends in the whole world or in any possible world, friends who understood me and didn't mind taking days and days out of their lives just so that I wouldn't end up crushed and beaten.

"I'll make it up to you," I said. "I'll paint sets, or I'll . . . I'll do what needs doing. Whatever it is. I'll go back home. I'll make up with Heather and play nice."

"Yes, you damn well will. But never mind that now," Ollie said. "We're going to California."

The others let out exhausted cheers.

We drove all the way to Albuquerque that day. It was a new thing for me, how quickly the landscape flew by us, patches of green changing to patches of red and yellow as the ground seemed to dry up under us.

"Cars go fast," I giggled with the kind of simplicity that comes from being either very drunk or very tired. Ollie floored the gas suddenly, and the old Buick sprang into action, sailing down the highway at a speed that made the girls shriek.

We got a hotel room that night, late enough that nobody wanted to drive any more, but almost as soon as we got up there Amy was fiddling around in back of the TV to hook up her DVD player.

"I just downloaded a torrent of this last night. It's so new it was subtitled by someone who barely even speaks English, but it's about a grim reaper and he's the guy in—you remember the one where everyone's in love tragically and they die prettily in the snow?"

"Oh, that guy," Lissa said. "He's yummy."

"Grim reaper, really?" Jon asked. "I thought we were full up on morbid over here."

"No," Amy argued. "It's a feel-good movie. He has a golden retriever."

We were all exhausted, but we didn't argue. Didn't even bother making token protests about getting up early in the morning. It just felt good, finally, to be together again. To go back to where the constants in life were bootleg movies and staying up too late. Even if we weren't talking about the things we needed to talk about yet, even if these friendships still had their brittle places, we had this. And we fell asleep in our clothes, warm and comfortable slouched on top of each other like newborn puppies.

The next day Ollie rallied us to hit the road early, determined to make it to the coast by night, but after we passed the state line the traffic started to snarl up around us—some idiot had managed to plow himself into a guard rail and swing out to obstruct two lanes of traffic. I felt somber; traffic accidents still made me think of Julia. And by the time we were past that snarl, we were well into the tangle of the morning commute from places like San Bernardino.

There was a kind of mystique to this place, to the sudden bursting out of civilization from all over the place (even if they did count shopping malls as civilization), and the greenness everywhere after the desert. Even if it was fake greenness kept up by endless lawn-watering.

We drove all the way up to where we could see the ocean glittering in the morning light. Ollie climbed out to explore while the rest of us lay dozing—and then, ten minutes later, he came back to the car and waved his arm for us to follow him, in the direction of the beach, the pier.

There was a little shop there called Surf 'N' Turf that rented out surfboards and roller skates and a couple of racks of beach cruisers, green and yellow old-fashioned bikes with big banana seats and streamers on the handlebars.

"You gotta cycle all the way to the shore," Ollie said. "It's only right."

We pooled our money, including my two dollars in change, and rented five bikes between us, and then we came down to the still mostly deserted beach and pedaled all the way down the wooden path that led up to the pier, squealing and chasing after each other. I squeezed myself down, trying to get myself into an aerodynamic position, and then started pedaling at an all-out clip, sailing past everyone else, and then they caught on and tried to keep up with me.

"That's not fair!" I heard behind me, and then, "Hey Lance, wait up!"

When a spray of sand caught me in the back I finally

gave up, circled around to give the rest of them a little head start, and let my pace slip to something more reasonable. As we neared the shore we got off our bikes and went down onto the sand. Then I could let my attention wander to other things: how the sea was both bright and gray at once, silvery and quiet. I saw people in shorts and bikinis trickling down to the shore, carrying surfboards and towels and paperbacks. A skinny kid with spikes of blond hair was stumbling forward, his nose stuck in a copy of *The Brothers Karamazov*. Someone had brought their poodles to the beach—big black beasts buried under curls of hair.

They saw us at the same moment that I saw them, and barreled toward us, red leashes snaking across the sand. We all screeched to a halt nearly at the same time, and it seems like we all fell onto each other in the sand—dogs, bikes, and us.

But once we'd untangled ourselves and were sitting together on the beach again, it was gloriously peaceful. Each of us seemed to hold on to a little piece of innocent childish silliness; Jon kept running into the surf and letting the waves chase him back out again. Amy bought an entirely too large bag of goodies from a shop on the boardwalk that sold old and obscure kinds of candy, and we were all dipping into it, eating nearly as much sand as candy in the process.

And Lissa started building a sand castle.

She worked slowly and carefully, packing sand into

place without any tools, shaping things that were be-
coming vaguely recognizable as walls, as towers.

And I knew what I was going to do.

"Ollie, can I have your keys?"

"Huh?"

"I need to grab something out of your car."

He tossed them to me. I shoved my sneakers back on
and rode my rented bike back to the car and grabbed
the two little boxes that I'd come for. Somehow it didn't
seem right to put them in a plastic bag and ride back
balancing them from the handlebars, so I settled for carrying them under one arm and walking the bike the long
way back to the beach, to the sand castle.

I knelt on the sand and removed objects one by one,
talking softly to myself.

"Aquaman lives in the castle." He balanced precari-
ously on the top of the building inside the walls.

"With Fishgirl," Lissa suggested, still touching up the
towers with little suggestions of turrets.

"Or Fishboy," Jon insisted.

"Either way. He has a car, which can drive underwater."

"A car?"

I carved out a little driveway and placed my little metal
car there. "It's okay because it runs on biodiesel."

I kept sticking things into the sand: hawk feather at
the top. Dried grass and corn husks and flowers lining the
outer walls. And, unexpected and out of place, there was
Julia's orange nail polish, grabbed at the last second,

which ought to have been in one of the bags that got stolen. I left in such a hurry that I hadn't even thought about what I was putting where, and—that was the only reason I still had it.

Oliver knelt down on the sand, reaching out toward these small things but hardly touching them, not taking a turn with the story.

"Fishgirl left Aquaman because he was cheating on her with Fishboy," Amy continued.

"Who was her twin brother," Jon added.

"Fine," I sighed, "hash out their dirty laundry for all the world to hear! It was a very painful experience for everyone involved."

"Not as painful as when Stingray went postal because his girlfriend got drunk at a party and started flashing people," Lissa said with a slight smirk.

"You don't want to mess with Stingray," Ollie added solemnly. And, finally, he smiled at me.

I kept up my interior decorating while they piled on the story, having come to the unstated consensus that the sordid—and increasingly gory, thanks to Amy—sea life soap opera was the most important thing in the world.

Just as they were describing in unfortunate detail the circumstances that led to Fishboy's tragic demise (which was in turn responsible for the neglectful and eccentric interior decorating), I put my last marble into place. I was done. And I moved on.

"Come over here," I called, moving out a little

toward the water. "I'm sure Fishboy didn't enjoy that fishhook through his eye, and the other places, but it can wait."

And they did.

I started digging a hole, and everyone else scooped out a little sand, until it was too large for a little breeze or wave to stir it up and fill it in.

The box that held Julia's ashes felt cool and feather-light in my hands. Oliver and Jon and Amy and Lissa were staring at me, waiting for me to make a move.

As I put the box into Oliver's hands, our fingers touched. I looked up at him, at those eyes I still could hardly meet, not sure if I could be forgiven for this crusade, and for taking the ashes. He answered me with a cautious nod, balancing it on his fingers like some fragile and dangerous thing, and gave it to Jon. We passed it around that circle once, and then put it down onto the sand.

That was where we poured out Julia's ashes. All of us, together, taking our turns in silence. Right between the sea and Aquaman's mansion. At the midpoint between us and our adolescent silliness, and the infinite that connected everything.

"You can see the ocean from here," I said.

"Waterfront property in SoCal," Amy commented. "That's hot."

And we had to laugh, because what else was there to do?

I cupped my hands around my mouth and threw my head up toward the sky.

"I love you!" I yelled.

I felt way too many eyes on me and looked down, more than a little embarrassed. "I had to make sure she could hear."

"Everyone within a forty-mile radius heard that, Cass," Jon said.

"Good." I realized that I was smiling, partly with shyness and partly with satisfaction.

Ollie was looking at me strangely—I couldn't tell if I was supposed to feel anxious or guilty or what. And then he grabbed me and pulled me into an awkward hug. We both loved her. And for the first time that felt like a bridge between us instead of a wall, like the biggest and most important thing we had ever shared.

"We're okay, you and me," he said directly. "You know that, right?"

"I shouldn't have—"

"Me neither."

I nodded. We were okay, and I could deal with going home, I could deal with facing Heather.

Me and Julia, we'd made it out here after all.

NOW

Wednesday night, the phone rang and I leaped for it.

"Cass?"

"Yeah." My heart fell when I heard Ollie on the line, after two days of hoping that it would be Heather.

"You realize it's Wednesday?"

"Yeah."

"You realize we open in two days?"

"We're ready. We're set. I've got nothing more to do."

"You couldn't find a better week to pick a fight with Heather?"

"Oh," I said.

"I'm not trying to pry into your personal life—"

"Then don't."

"But if we do not have a lead, we do not have much of a play. And right now we have a lead who would rather be spectacularly mopey than be a ninja princess. And there's only, like, three minutes of spectacularly mopey in the script."

"And that's supposed to be my fault?"

"I don't know," Ollie admitted. "Nobody seems to want to tell me anything, and I know better than to listen to rumors, and maybe she's miserable because her puppy died or something—"

"Iguana," I said quietly. "She's allergic. She wants an iguana."

"And if that would make her give a halfway convincing performance, I would buy her an iguana. Just fix it, okay? Please?"

I sighed. "Why does it have to be my fault?"

"I don't know whose fault it is. I don't care whose fault it is. I just don't want to deal with it anymore, and in case you're wondering, Heather got the same lecture."

But she hadn't done anything about it yet.

"Oliver, I don't know how to fix this. If I had even the slightest idea, I would be over there in ten seconds to say the right things and do the right things and make everything okay again. I'm lost here."

"Say the wrong things, then, as long as you can say them by Friday."

But I couldn't. I already knew I couldn't.

I did not know what to do.

I came at it from every angle, gnawed at it in class and when I was trying to get to sleep, but I didn't get anywhere. I couldn't even seem to find a foothold.

If Julia were here, I'd call her and she'd come over and she would know what to do, and even if she didn't, she would try to cheer me up and I would manage to be cheered up by her trying.

It had been so long since I'd talked to her.

Friday afternoon I needed something to do, to distract me from the play that night, which I would not be going to see. If it was going to be a disaster, and if it was going to be my fault, I didn't want to be anywhere nearby. Instead, I rode to the chichi grocery store, the one that played classical music and sold organic everything, and picked up a little bunch of lilies and daisies in white and pink and yellow. And I went down to the cemetery.

Even though Julia had been cremated, she still had a little memorial stone there, beside her grandmother.

"Hey," I said nervously. I had so much to tell her. And I didn't have a clue how to start.

My backpack felt way too heavy, and I shrugged it

off my shoulders, then remembered why it was so heavy. *Totally Sweet Ninja Death Squad*, lyrics and music, worn out at the corners from being dragged around in my backpack and read and reread. I smoothed it out, flipped through the pages. "I'm sorry," I said. "I didn't mean to screw this up for you. I didn't even mean to get involved in the first place. I just wish that you were still around and we could argue about whether ninjas can actually divide by zero."

I put my flowers down on her headstone and sat on my knees and hung my head low so that she could hear me.

"Julia? You remember when we promised each other that we'd be each other's maids of honor? You remember when you told me that I would fall in love someday and I would love it and I would hate it and I'd eventually feel like punching someone in the face over it? You remember when someone made some stupid comment about me being gay, and you grinned and laughed it off as if—as if it wasn't an insult to think that we might be girlfriends, you and me?"

Of course she remembered, and knew, and understood.

"Julia, I like a girl. Who isn't you. I mean, I like you, but I like somebody else too."

I wished that I had her to talk to, in real life. Wished that I could have told her I loved her more, when I was too frightened to, because it was saying too many things I wasn't sure about.

But she would have understood.

I believed that as much as I'd ever believed anything.

"So, look—if I didn't say anything when you were alive, it wasn't because I didn't trust you, or because I was afraid. It was because I didn't understand it myself, and—more than that, it's because what we had was always way beyond words. It's like what Heather said about poems. They're not for understanding. You just listen to them, and you let your heart beat in time with their music, and that's all you need. I'm not sorry. I can't ever regret anything about what was between us.

"I think maybe I'm going to have a girlfriend now. If we can get past this. If we can work it out. And I think maybe you'd be the one telling me every dumb joke you knew until I worked out how to make it better.

"Hey, Julia, what do you call cheese that isn't yours? Nacho cheese!"

I lay there in the autumn sun, full of the smell of rich wet dirt and daisies and lilies, and I told Julia that I liked Heather, yeah, the same Heather we *haaated* in middle school, and was that okay? I told her that Heather had kissed me in the library, and that she had played the clarinet for me under my window, and that she had taken me out for French pastries and told me I was pretty. And she was in the play that Julia wrote, and she was going to be wonderful, because she was small and graceful and silly and sarcastic and sincere.

"I have to go," I said. "I have to go find her and make

things right somehow. I have to give her these flowers."

I knelt on the dirt and lowered my head again, touching my forehead to the ground, and then my lips. I brushed the dirt off the petals, off my pants.

"I love you, Julia. Ever since third grade, I've loved you. But I think I have to love somebody else too."

One lily for Julia, on her headstone. The rest went in the white wicker basket on my old bike. I checked my watch—six, an hour till curtains—and sped toward the school.

It was almost too late for secrecy now, so Mr. Vaichon was there with the ninja extras handing out programs, who were about to get slaughtered in the first scene. I filed backstage, toward the classrooms that had been set up for dressing rooms.

When I knocked at the first one I came to, Jon ducked out of the door. "Girls are down the hall, one forty-three," he said. "Good luck."

"Since when does everybody know way too much about my life?"

"It's called friendship. Get used to it."

I stood in front of 143. I was smudged with dirt—my flowers were smudged with dirt. But I was running out of time. I knocked. And I knocked.

"We're getting dressed," someone yelled.

"I just need to talk to Heather!"

"She's getting dressed."

"Yeah, but—"

"I don't want to talk to you," Heather's voice called out.

"Please, just for a minute. It can't wait."

I heard something behind the door—a lot of quick, quiet talking I couldn't make out—and then the door opened and Heather came out, looking entirely unhappy, done up in a full black-and-red kimono tied with a butterfly sash at the waist, hair hanging straight down her back.

"I have to go on in like, three minutes, and I'm trying really hard just to keep it together, and you're not helping by just showing up here with flowers—"

"I know."

"You're smudgy."

"I know." I wiped at my face with the back of my hand, but I doubted it made much difference. "I had to go down to the cemetery and talk to Julia. Because I know I was being stupid, and I was being stupid because I hadn't talked to her about you yet."

"That's what this is about?" Nothing sarcastic in that question, or contemptuous. Just a question.

"I know it sounds silly, but if we are even going to be friends, you can't be making fun of my stupid dead girlfriend."

She looked at me, quiet, for a long time, and barely nodded.

"I like you, a lot. And I trust you, a lot, or I wouldn't have told you that."

"Look," she said. "I've been through the wringer of breaking up and getting back together and breaking up and getting back together. Don't do that to me." But her shoulders relaxed, and her frown lightened a little.

"I won't."

"And if you're going to be my girlfriend, you have to be my girlfriend. Not my lab partner, not my math tutor, not my friend, my girlfriend. In public. Even when it's scary. It is for me too."

"I'd shout it from the rooftops."

"Better not," she said, the sadness in her face cracking open at last. "I'm still not telling Gran, because she would have a heart attack, and Alex and Noah because my sister says they're too young, and if we ever happen to run into one of the nuns from St. Joseph's we're not together, but . . . everywhere else is okay . . ."

That was when I kissed her. I leaned down over her and covered her mouth with mine, touching my hand to the bare curve of her shoulder blade to pull her closer. We parted trembling, nearly frozen in place.

"No rooftops. Check."

We could've stayed there all night, but the classroom door swung open and Amy stared at us. "Um, hi? Not to interrupt you two, but we're going on in five minutes, remember?"

"Five minutes figuratively or five minutes literally?" Heather asked.

"Literally!"

"Okay, okay, okay, I'm coming," Heather insisted.

I went back to the auditorium with my legs feeling cold and weak. Good, but like my heart was worn out and exhausted.

I nearly missed Ollie when I passed him in the hallway—he had to reach out and grab my arm before I saw him.

"What are you doing here?"

"Watching a play," I said innocently. "I heard *Our Town* was a masterpiece of drama."

"Is there anything you wanted to tell me?"

"Ask me later. I gotta run and get a seat. I'm hoping for something in the blood-spray rows."

He shook his head.

The auditorium was packed. There's nothing like good gossip to fill the seats, and we had enough of that to go around—not just that we were putting on *Totally Sweet Ninja Death Squad* instead of *Our Town,* but that the lead had broken up with her girlfriend and it was going to be a complete train wreck. People love a good train wreck. And they seemed to love the signs sternly warning people from sitting in the first three rows if they did not want to get splattered with corn syrup.

Those rows were full.

Hunting for a seat, I realized that someone was waving

at me—and there, near the front but just outside of the blood-spray rows, my parents had saved me a place between them and Julia's mom.

Even though I'd said I wasn't coming.

"Are you sure you want to be here?" I said. "It's kind of violent."

"I'm not expecting a play called *Totally Sweet Ninja Death Squad* to be particularly peaceful," Mom said matter-of-factly. "Don't we always go see Julia's plays?"

And we did, so that settled it.

"Isn't that a girl you know?" she murmured, looking at the playbill. "Heather Galloway?"

"You might have heard me complaining about her three or four dozen times in eighth grade."

"That's where I remember her name from!" She looked at me with concern.

I was trying to be casual, but the words ended up tumbling out in a pile. "And by the way, is it okay if she comes over for dinner sometime?"

"I don't see why not."

And I wondered if she knew more than she ever said she knew. If she wanted me to have more space to make my own mistakes and my own discoveries than I even had by myself on the open road.

There were a lot of things I had never said anything about. Almost everything that happened over the summer, everything that happened in Missouri. But I thought that I could start talking now.

It was seven minutes past six, and everyone had put away their playbills and started playing games on their cell phones. Out of habit, rummaging through my backpack to see if I had something to read, my hand closed over something that I recognized right away. I turned to Julia's mom.

"Sheila," I said. "This probably sounds kind of strange, but he came to California with us, and—I think you should have it."

A little plastic Aquaman, chewed and battered from being thrown out of a minivan window long before I ever picked him up off the highway. "It doesn't necessarily make sense," I said.

She took it as if it was a mysterious relic, and passed it over quietly to Julia's dad. "I'm not sure that singing, dancing ninjas make sense. It doesn't necessarily have to make sense."

I smiled, and I thought again about what Heather had said about poetry. How it was okay for things not to make sense.

At fifteen minutes past six, even I was starting to get twitchy. Somebody yelled out, "I want ninjas!" and someone else yelled out, "*Our Town* isn't supposed to have ninjas!" and I didn't know if they were in on the joke or not, but another person yelled out, "Ninjas!"

"Ninjas!"

A figure stepped out from the curtains, all in black and nearly invisible, holding out a sword that looked convincing, at least from this distance. "There will be silence," he said.

And there was.

And the curtain went up, and Loud Ninja and Buddhist Ninja and Flamboyant Ninja appeared in the woods, Loud Ninja bragging about how great ninjas were and squeaking out the high notes of "Ninjas Can Divide By Zero."

The shogun's army fell on them just as they finished singing, and the slaughter began. Blood was spurting stylishly all over, and everything was a confusion of black with glints of silver, and the orchestra started to swell up, and—it was perfect. It was real.

Ninja Princess Himiko started to fall in love with Hiromasa, and I recognized her, anxious and guarded and fierce and then grinning like everything was going to be all right. Still not trusting him all the way, though, until Hiromasa managed to smuggle out plans to the booby-trapped castle—only to discover that Loud Ninja and Buddhist Ninja, attempting to spy on him, had been captured. Hiromasa realized that the terrible rule of the shogun justified the rebellion, and the ninjas had been right all along, and as he sang "Loyalty Is Overrated," he and Himiko started to plan a raid on a castle to free the captured righteous.

This was my turn. Hiromasa and Himiko sneaked through the castle. Trapdoors opened under their feet, arrows flew just barely over their heads, and as shurikens flew out of a wall toward them Himiko caught them without missing a beat. And I forgot I was watching Heather and Oliver dressed up, and it faded into this story that was strange and slightly ridiculous and above all else beautiful.

It was perfect, in its imperfections, in the way that Jon fell over himself in the middle of a fight scene and ad-libbed "Live by the sword, trip and fall on the sword" into his song five minutes later, in the way that Heather's singing voice was thin and chirpy and just right. And then near the beginning of the second act, that little scene where Himiko—now almost despondent about having vowed revenge on Hiromasa, because she was falling in love with him—sang,

> *"The flavor of blood is sadness,*
> *And also a little like copper and salt.*
> *Revenge is as bitter as unripe persimmons,*
> *Even when you know who's at fault."*

And Hiromasa, unseen till now, stepped out of the trees.

> *"You think that love is weakness,*
> *You think that you'll die if you show any doubt,*
> *But living and fighting for what you love*
> *Is never the coward's way out."*

And they just stared at each other, finally realizing that

they loved each other, finally realizing that this was bigger than who killed who—and Heather shot a sideways glance toward the audience, the kind of glance that said "By the way, this kiss is for you." And when she kissed him I nearly fell out of my chair.

It ended as happily as you could hope for. It ended with everybody deciding to bring down the shogun together, and singing a rousing chorus about their doomed mission. Sometime in the last few months I'd grown strangely fond of doomed missions.

I told my parents I'd be home a little late and then ran down to join them, and we all swarmed out into the courtyard, still costumed. Jon hooked his iPod up to a big stereo. The courtyard filled with electronica, three dozen ninjas waving back and forth in time.

We found Ollie, who had a dazed, self-satisfied smile on his face.

"It was a pretty unconventional production of *Our Town*," he said. "So I got a week of detention. I think that's enough time to start working on *Rosencrantz and Guildenstern Are Zombies* . . ."

"What about Mr. Vaichon?"

"I managed to persuade the principal that he would never have allowed it if he had known anything about it, and we were just too convincing in our volunteer efforts with *Our Town*. It helps that we actually have evidence that we helped out with it."

Heather grabbed a berry lemonade and dragged me

along until we could hear ourselves think. We leaned against the side of the school and took turns taking sips from the bottle.

"So you talked to Julia about us."

"Yeah."

"Did she approve?"

"Oh, yeah, sure. Absolutely," I said. It could have stung, but she said it as a perfectly serious question.

She smirked, looked up, and waved vaguely in the direction of the sky. "Okay, now I don't so much want to think about her watching us."

I rolled my eyes. "Like I didn't hear about twice as much as I really needed to know about her and Ollie. It's only fair."

I smirked, and she smirked back at me.

"You want to take off, before we get busted for having a ninja rave on school grounds?"

"Definitely." And then I had a crazy little idea.

"I'll give you a ride."

"In what car?"

"On my bike. Riding double. I've done it a ton of times."

"That's not safe," Heather said. "Is it?"

"Trust me."

She hesitated a moment. "Good enough."

I unlocked my pink bike, and we loaded things in the

panniers—the lock, her clothes, her flowers, a very carefully balanced half-finished bottle of lemonade. I hauled my bike right to the top of the hill, and got on in front. Heather squeezed in on the back half of the saddle, feet on the chain stays, her hands wrapped tight around my waist, her chest leaning close against my back.

I checked the weight, checked the balance—yeah. Safe. As much as we can ever be.

Then, with just the slightest touch against the pavement, the bike took off. It was too small for me, it put my knees at weird angles and the derailleur complained on the higher gears, but on a steep enough downhill it didn't matter.

I changed up to a higher gear, and a higher one, and pedaled like mad just to see how fast we could get—and the wind and gravity caught us. I yelled into the air from exhilaration. And Heather yelled up into the air too, a high "Wheee!" that probably carried for miles. Then the hill bottomed out, and I had to switch back to the lowest gear and pedal with all my strength. In the dark-blue night, with my headlight blinking on and off, with Heather's cheek pressed right up against my neck, I felt the heartbeat of the world. Like everything alive was as close to me as the touch of skin on the back of my neck. And Julia too. Julia, always.

And I didn't care if the whole world knew it.

A NOVEL

★ A LOVE STORY ★

THANK
YOU

THANKS

To my editor, Alisha Niehaus, for all her hard work in making this book stronger.

Thanks to my entire family, especially to my mom and my sister Meaghan for advice, moral support, and driving a U-Haul halfway across Brooklyn. Thanks to Brian Sturm for all he taught me about telling stories.

Thanks to the late Ken Kifer for his passionate essays on bicycle camping and bicycle advocacy, which first bewitched me with the idea of a girl and a bicycle and a very long journey.